Lifting her without effort, Cortez placed her on the countertop and made quick work of the button-down bodice of the curve-hugging dress she was wearing. Once the tiny row of pearl buttons was undone, he brought his persuasive lips to the valley between her breasts. Strong teeth tugged at the front of her dress as it was pulled away to reveal her chest.

Cortez leaned back and studied the round, flawless dark globes with hungry eyes. He licked his lips before settling them to the tip of one mound. Closing his eyes, he savored the sweet, familiar taste of her skin.

Julia's weak cry filled the kitchen when she felt the passionate nibbling on her nipples. She arched her back, pushing more of herself into Cortez's hot mouth.

"Mmm…" Cortez moaned when he felt the slight movement. Pushing her dress off her shoulders, his fingers caressed her bare skin and pulled her even closer.

Shivers of delight danced along Julia's spine and she gasped. Throwing her head back, she threw her doubts and caution and questions aside. She was sick of fighting and ready to take what she wanted.

Books by AlTonya Washington

Kimani Romance

A Lover's Pretense
A Lover's Mask
Pride and Consequence
Rival's Desire
Hudson's Crossing
The Doctor's Private Visit
As Good as the First Time

Kimani Arabesque

Remember Love
Guarded Love
Finding Love Again
Love Scheme
A Lover's Dream

ALTONYA WASHINGTON

has many titles; aside from Mom, her favorite is romance author. Crafting stories and characters that are sexy and engaging with a fair amount of mystery really keeps her busy. When AlTonya's not writing, she works as a library assistant and as social secretary to an active son—a job that commands the bulk of her time. Visit her Web site at www.lovealtonya.com or e-mail her at altonya@lovealtonya.com.

As **GOOD** As the First Time

ALTONYA WASHINGTON

To the readers. I am continually blessed and
motivated by your awesome support!

KIMANI PRESS™

Recycling programs
for this product may
not exist in your area.

ISBN-13: 978-0-373-86171-2

AS GOOD AS THE FIRST TIME

Dear Reader,

I hope that you'll enjoy my latest super sexy effort. This time we're jet-setting between Detroit and Los Angeles for what I hope you'll find to be a romantically sensual treat.

I'm sure we've all wondered from time to time about the one who got away. Our heroine Julia Kelly is about to find out what happens when she puts her wondering into effect. The road is going to be a rocky one, but once you've met our hero Cortez Wallace, I think you'll understand why she chooses to take it!

This story has gone through lots of changes since I first drafted it in 1998. That's right! It was 1998 was when I first had the idea for Julia and her sinfully seductive ex. I'm proud to say that the characters have really evolved since that first draft. Additionally, the heat, intensity and edge that I love to bring to my stories is in full gear amidst the pages you're about to begin.

So settle down, curl up and lose yourself in *As Good as the First Time*.

Enjoy the romance,

Al

Prologue

"How'd you get into this thing?"

"Don't you know? You were watching me get dressed the entire time."

"I was more concerned with getting you out of it."

"I remember."

The soft whispers of suggestive conversation drifted into silence. Julia Kelly wound her slender arms around Cortez Wallace's neck and met the lustful thrusts of his tongue inside her mouth with her own brand of sweet pleasure. Once again, the elevator car was filled with only the sounds of feminine cries of delight and the unmistakable moans of male satisfaction.

Cortez groaned each time her tongue swirled around his own and he hoisted her securely against his athletic frame. Caught up in their passion, the couple never wondered when—or even if—anyone would encroach upon their lovers' tryst. After all, an elevator wasn't the most private of places. They thrived as much upon the possibility of discovery as they did on the enjoyment of privacy.

Cortez held Julia trapped in one corner of the car, tearing his mouth from hers to settle it at the pulse point of her throat. He felt her seeking hands at the belt around his black trousers and folded his larger hands over hers when she sought to tug down his zipper.

"Haven't you had enough of having fun in public?" Cortez asked, taking hold of her wrists and pressing them near her sides against the paneled elevator walls.

"Have *you?*" Julia teased, tugging her bottom lip between her teeth. She ground her body against him and felt the stiff muscle straining against his pants. "Besides, your mother got what she deserved," she added, recalling Cora Wallace's look of horror and distaste when she walked in on Cortez and Julia "carrying on" in one of the deserted corridors of the restaurant where they'd all met for dinner that evening. A shuddery moan lilted from Julia's throat when his lips fastened to her earlobe and he lightly suckled.

"Give her a break," Cortez chided, his big hands cupping Julia's bottom to settle her more snugly against him.

"Mmm," Julia sighed, wrapping her long, dark legs around his waist. "She only came to spy on us, you know," Julia said. "She had absolutely no business in that part of the restaurant." Julia's lashes fluttered as Cortez's hand disappeared inside the scooping bodice of her gown to fondle an aching nipple.

His handsome caramel-toned face followed the path of his hand as he nuzzled into her ample boson. "Julia,

I really don't want to discuss my mother just now." His tone was matter-of-fact. "In fact, I don't want to *discuss* at all," he decided, just as his mouth captured the nipple that wasn't being manipulated by his fingers.

Julia had no qualms. Airily, she acknowledged for the hundredth time that she'd never have Cora Wallace's approval no matter what she did.

Julia and Cortez managed to set their clothes right before the elevator opened on the floor to the apartment they shared. The front door opened to them kissing again madly. Cortez kicked the door shut while Julia worked on the collar of the stark white shirt he wore with his tux. He'd undone his tie long ago and cast it to the backseat of his Pathfinder.

Their clothes flew all over the living room amidst their frenzied disrobing. Julia raked her French tips across the light beard Cortez had taken to wearing over the last several months.

"Tsk, tsk. I was just getting used to this," she lamented, trailing her tongue across the sleek black whiskers covering his square jaw. "Now you'll have to let it go for the job," she said, referring to his first anchor position at WPDM-TV.

The promotion was cause for the celebratory dinner earlier that night. Much of Cortez's family was in attendance. Julia had hoped her family would join the celebration, as well. She'd been promptly informed that they would just as soon break bread with a pack of rabid wolves than dine with the uppity Wallace clan.

Unlike the humble presence Julia's family held in the Detroit area, Cortez's family was quite well-known. Aside from Cortez's prominence as the area's most popular broadcaster (and most sought after bachelor), his brother,

Correll Wallace, owned a high-profile advertising agency. Correll began his business with inheritance money from his and Cortez's deceased father. Andre Wallace's array of car dealerships across the Motor City earned him a highly prominent and respected name.

"I don't plan on letting it go," Cortez said, pushing Julia's ankle-length curve-tugging black gown down over her hips. "It's why I got the job."

"Liar," Julia accused playfully, splaying her hands across the rigid pack of muscles lining his abdomen.

"I can prove it. Delia told me she loved it."

"Oh Delia," Julia sighed, repeating the name of the only female executive at the station. "I'm not surprised. She just wants to sleep with you."

"Shame on you, talkin' that way about our superior," Cortez teased, now kneeling before her and removing her black lace panties with his teeth.

Julia let out a delighted shriek when his tongue barely brushed the throbbing flesh of her femininity. "Mmm... my superior—now *your* equal," she managed to correct him.

Cortez rested his forehead against her thigh for a moment before he stood. "You deserve to be right next to me in that broadcast booth," he said as he pulled her tightly against him.

Julia shook her head, sending locks of her glossy dark bob into her face. "I prefer behind-the-scenes work," she said, referring to her position as production assistant for the station where she'd worked alongside Cortez before his promotion. "I don't think I'm cut out to work in front of the camera."

"With this face?" Cortez countered, giving her a slight shake. "And if they could see this body..." he started, his deep brown eyes raking past her collarbone before he hefted her against his bare chest. "In front of a camera is exactly where you should be. There, or walking down an aisle to become my wife."

Julia's gaze fell. "Corky..."

He nodded, already knowing what she was thinking. He'd asked more than a few times during the four years they'd lived together. She'd always refused, saying she liked them the way they were. He'd argued against her resistance while she continued to resist. Eventually he realized he loved her too much to make a real issue out of it.

"Like I said, in front of the camera, nowhere else." He returned the lightness to their banter.

"Oh, Corky," Julia sighed playfully, relief filling her eyes when they fixed on the seductive curve of his mouth, "when will you anchor types realize that the power is *behind* the lights?"

Cortez began to knead her bottom in his wide palms. "Power, huh?" he probed.

"Mmm, hmm that's what I want—what I crave."

"Only at the station?"

Julia cupped the back of his head and smoothed her fingers across his soft hair where it tapered at his neck. "Only everywhere," she clarified with a devilish grin.

Words were unnecessary and undesired after that. The heated talking and caressing resumed. Julia met the force and savagery of his kiss with her own special fire. The muscles flexed involuntarily in Cortez's arms as he held her close and headed toward their bedroom.

Much later in the night, Julia awoke and stretched languidly. She was completely satisfied, as she always was after making love with Cortez. In the distance, however, she could hear voices, and they were angry ones. Whipping back the covers, Julia grabbed her robe from an armchair and headed out of the bedroom. She found Cortez in the living room with Correll Wallace. Under no circumstances would she have eavesdropped, except for the fact that Cortez and his older brother never argued. Then she heard her name in the midst of the heated conversation.

"...do you know how upset she was after seeing that?"

"What the hell was she doing there anyway?"

Correll fixed his brother with an exasperated look. Clearly he felt their mother's snooping was justified in light of what she'd walked in on between Cortez and Julia. "It doesn't matter where Ma was. You and your girl should learn how to keep your...love scenes private."

"Well, here we are in our own home, so why don't you go run and tell Ma that?" Cortez snapped, strolling toward the front door.

Correll intended to have his say. "She's beneath you, man," he said in the coolest of tones.

Cortez clenched his jaw, feeling his simmering temper heat to boil. "Get out, Correll," he warned.

"She's got no restraint. She does what she wants when she wants and doesn't care who sees it."

"Correll—"

"Hell, Tez, she's almost straight out of the projects. She didn't even attend a real college—put herself through some night school—"

"And came out with a degree just as good as ours," Cortez roared, shoving his hands into the deep pockets of his black sleep pants. "You forget she's the golden girl at the station. If they could get away with it, they wouldn't even hire other production assistants. She's that damn good at her job."

"It's her actions, man," Correll persisted, folding his arms over the front of his now slightly wrinkled tuxedo jacket. "Out in a restaurant messin' around like that? She's got no self-control, Tez."

"She wasn't there alone," Cortez reminded his brother.

Correll seemed happy he'd broached the subject, "Well let's talk about that, too. Hell, man, you're about to be very well-known. You can't afford someone like her giving you that sort of reputation."

Cortez stepped away from the front door, his dark eyes narrowed to thin slits. "What reputation?" he asked, whispering purposefully.

"The kind she's had since high school. You think a woman who looks like that isn't getting offers from every fool out there? And I'll bet she's taking as many as she can get."

Cortez closed the distance between himself and Correll. "Correll, you'd better leave on your own now or I swear you won't be able to," he threatened, glaring deep into his brother's eyes.

Correll blinked, seeing something in his sibling's expression that made him reconsider his next words. "Tez, you know what I'm talking about here."

"I know what Ma's been fillin' your head with. Hell, you sound just like her. Reputation?" Cortez's stare narrowed even farther. "Why? Because she's never had a problem talking to a man with honesty and sensibility instead of letting him think her IQ's smaller than her breast size?"

Correll broke eye contact with his brother, knowing his accusations were unfounded. Julia was practically obsessed with Cortez. Still, that wouldn't make him take back what he'd just said. "Watch her, Tez," he added with a cold stare.

"You come to me with this crap about Julia again and we never see each other again, simple as that," Cortez promised, walking toward the door, which he then held open for Correll.

Julia had lost sight of Cortez and his brother minutes ago. Her eyes were too blurred by tears to see anything properly. Hearing Correll Wallace's words wasn't the cause of her tears—his mother had said things far uglier. Of course, the outbursts were always spoken out of Cortez's presence.

Seeing him standing there, hearing all those terrible opinions—*that* she could not take. Correll was right about one thing: Cortez didn't need that sort of drama if he was going to be in the public eye. She would always be Julia Kelly. Julia Kelly from the wrong income bracket. Julia Kelly who went to night school instead of a great HBCU. Julia Kelly who *carried on* in restaurant corridors. Julia Kelly—the kind of woman no mother wanted her son involved with.

She'd hurried back to bed by the time Cortez slammed the door behind his brother. She pretended to be asleep when he slid into bed next to her. Once Cortez finally drifted off to sleep, she turned to look at him, taking in the handsome, deep caramel-toned face that would soon be gracing televisions all over Detroit. Swallowing a sob, she leaned close to brush her lips across his temple. She dreaded what she was about to do, but she needed to do it just the same.

Chapter 1

Detroit, 2010

Cortez Wallace had changed drastically in the last eight years. He'd gone from an unknown entity to one of the most powerful and respected anchors in the industry. True, his journalistic prowess helped him garner a fair share of the accolades. But everyone knew his sinfully handsome features were the real asset. Women blatantly admitted that a man like Cortez Wallace made even the most heinous news story a pleasure to hear.

That morning, however, Cortez was feeling anything but pleasure. A scowl contorted his face as he bounded down the corridor to his office suite. In his eight years working for WPDM, he'd never been so eager to leave.

Cortez's assistant, Sara McBride, saw her boss on his way down the hall, and her smile widened with a syrupy sweetness that gained in intensity the closer he came to her desk.

* * *

"There he is," Sara sang, only to earn a sinister glare from the man who stormed past her.

Cortez stopped just before entering his office. Hands braced on either side of the doorway, he bowed his head. "Sara, come in here, please," he said without turning to look at her.

Sara's smile disappeared in a flash. She bit her lip while standing up to do as he'd asked.

"What's going on around here?" he demanded to know, rolling up the sleeves of his midnight blue shirt to reveal muscular forearms. "I mean, I feel like I'm on a sugar high with everybody being so sweet to me. What? Have I been given six months to live and everyone knows but me?"

Sara watched him in disbelief as she took a few steps toward to his desk. "Well, haven't you seen the society page this morning?"

The way she phrased the question, as though she were asking if he'd had coffee with his breakfast, set Cortez's scowl even more firmly in place. "The society page," he said, stroking his light beard as though he were making an effort to recall. "My chances of seeing it are about as likely as my decorating a wedding cake, I'm afraid."

Sara tapped a nail to her berry-colored lips and grinned. "It's funny you should mention wedding cake."

"I'm losin' patience, Sara."

Quickly, Sara extended her hands and made a move for the door. "Sorry, Cortez, just hold on a minute, all right?" she asked, racing out the office. She returned some ten seconds later carrying a newspaper.

"The society page, I presume?" Cortez inquired dryly as he leaned against the edge of his desk.

"The article's circled," Sara told him as she passed him the paper.

Cortez scanned the article that had been ringed with hot pink highlighter. After a few seconds of reading, muttered curses spilled past his lips and the paper crinkled as his grip upon it tightened. "What the hell?" he bellowed finally, causing his assistant to jump. When he tossed the paper aside and looked up, Sara was already at the entrance to the office.

"Get her in here," he ordered, massaging his neck as he stood.

Los Angeles

"This is a joke, right?" Julia Kelly calmly inquired of the five men seated in the conference room. Her expression, however, spoke volumes and said that she knew they were dead serious.

James Sealy, vice president of programming for Outlook TV, leaned forward over the cherry-wood table. "Julia, I'm asking," he said—*though it sounded close to begging*— "to please go along with us on this. It's a good idea and we want to see it through."

But you want to keep me happy, too, Julia thought silently. The last thing the popular cable network wanted to do was lose their hottest producer. Of course, she wasn't nice enough to let them off the hook so easily. "I suppose you four have forgotten," she began, glaring at the executives seated before her, "that I came to you four months ago with a similar idea of my own?" she asked, watching the men fidget in their seats before she turned to the fifth man in the room, Kenrick Owens.

"No offense, Ken," she apologized unsympathetically, before turning on the executives once more, "but my idea is far more fresh, and besides, I've got years more experience." She recrossed her long legs, which were covered by silver-gray trousers. "My show is a few steps beyond your investigative exposés. It brings the public to the places in L.A. they wouldn't go if their lives depended on it. By bringing attention to these places, improvements could be possible. Change could be affected. Real change." One silver-gray-and-black pump dangled as she crisply relayed her pitch. "I'm not only offering a voyeuristic peek into L.A.'s seedy side, guys. I'm offering hope for improvement. Not to mention the fact that my host is a *woman*." Julia's dark eyes narrowed then as though she'd just made the discovery of the century. "Now, that couldn't possibly be the reason you guys are giving it the boot?"

"We are not giving it the boot," James promised, tugging nervously at his collar, "we only want to try Ken's approach first."

"Right," Julia sighed, setting her elbows on the arms of the chair she occupied and lacing her fingers together. "That's right, give the men a go first, since it's got real potential. Then, if it fails, give the little girls a shot."

At once the men began to plead and insist that she was wrong. It was obvious how determined they were to have her on board.

"Enough, enough," she urged, casually raking her fingers through glossy, jet-black locks that she now wore in a gorgeous boyish cut. "Don't worry, fellas, I'm not gonna run home crying and then turn in my resignation because I've been screwed. If that were the case, I doubt you'd have one woman left working at this damned network."

"Julia, wait!" Bennett Daniels, Outlook's public relations and marketing vice president, called when she got up to leave. "We need you to do more than just go along with us on this."

Julia turned, propping a hand on the banded waistband of her chic cuffed trousers. "What? You want me to rework Ken's concept and write the show's copy, too?"

Sounds of cleared throats and sighs filled the room and drowned before Ben continued.

"We have several candidates in mind for this thing, Julia, but there's only one we're highly interested in. Trouble is, he's the top man at a respected station in Detroit."

Julia pulled her hand from her hip and stepped closer to the conference table at the mention of her hometown. Her silence prompted Ben to continue.

"We want Cortez Wallace in the top spot."

Julia almost lost her ability to stand. Thankfully, no one seemed to notice her unease.

"We know you and Cortez were acquainted," James said. "So we figured that since you two know each other..."

"What? You just figured on having me charm him to get him to sign on?"

"Damn it, Julia!" James spat, while his colleagues uttered similar responses at her insinuation. "Just calm down, because the attitude is not necessary."

"Oh no, James?" Julia challenged, glaring into his reddened face. "Not even when you guys shoot down my idea and then ask me to help you make the show you really want instead?"

"Would you just *think* about it?" Bennett urged. "Kenrick's already agreed to give you coproducer rights if you just meet with Cortez when he decides to come out for a visit."

Julia froze, her dark, oval face a picture of stunned unease. "He-he's coming out here?"

Again, the group shuffled restlessly in their seats.

"He hasn't agreed yet," James admitted, "but he did sound intrigued by the possibility. Besides, he's been with WPDM for almost ten years, and we're hoping he's ready for a change. He knows you, and a familiar face may make the possibility of relocating more appealing."

Hmph, Julia mused. Her *face* wasn't the only thing Cortez Wallace was familiar with. How many times had he run across her mind during the last eight years? She'd forbidden herself to even tune in to the online broadcasts from Detroit. She never asked about him when she spoke with family or friends. She'd finally succeeded in safely tucking him away in the deepest recesses of her past, right?

"Julia?"

She realized they were all watching her expectantly. In a soft, demure and completely un-Julia-like way, she smiled and nodded. "Um…could I just have some time to think about it?" she asked.

The guys exchanged uncertain glances and nodded slowly. Clearly, they couldn't believe she'd even agreed to do that. Julia said nothing more and left the conference room shortly afterward.

When the door closed behind her, Ben's eyes fluttered closed as he massaged the bridge of his nose.

Matthew Henderson, another executive who'd been present at the meeting, had decided to play it safe by not speaking. "Damn, she's one tough woman," he let out finally.

James shook his head. "Makes you wonder what she's like in bed," he quipped, smiling as each man quietly uttered words of agreement while happily envisioning that very idea.

"What the hell are you doing giving comments like this?" Cortez demanded when Renee Scales stood in his office twenty minutes after he'd asked to see her.

"I don't see what the problem is," she responded in her vaguely haughty manner. Folding her arms across the front of her smart, peach skirt suit, she appeared cool and poised—her usual demeanor. "We *have* been seeing each other several months—"

"Those were business dinners to discuss stories," he corrected. "And now we're engaged?" Cortez asked, as though seeking clarification for something he felt was utterly preposterous.

Renee rolled her light eyes. "It says nothing like that," she said and waved airily at the article now lying crumpled on Cortez's desk. "Of course, it *does* leave the impression that we're in a committed relationship and that an engagement may be on the horizon...unless you have issues with that phrase?"

Cortez frowned. "Unless it says 'committed to work,' you're damn straight I've got issues with it. And there is most certainly no engagement on the horizon."

Renee shrugged nonchalantly, though the look in her eyes was one of distinct uneasiness.

Cortez was so in awe of the situation that he couldn't grasp any of it. "Listen, Renee," he sighed, sounding as though he were struggling to maintain his calm. "We're public people, and comments like this can easily be misconstrued. We're reporters, and you know we don't need much to run with, even if it *is* a lie."

The look on Renee's attractive café-au-lait face grew

stormy. "So our relationship is all business, nothing else at all?"

Cortez's groan almost smothered the sound of his phone ringing. *How the devil had a few meals in public turned into this?* he marveled. "Wallace," he said as he answered the call.

"I'm very upset with you." Cora Wallace's high-pitched, nasal tone drifted through the receiver. "But I'll forgive you as soon as you tell me when this engagement will be made formal."

Instead of responding to his mother's inquiry, Cortez stood. "It's for you," he told Renee, and he passed the phone to her before he left his office.

He can't come here, he just can't, Julia had been thinking since she left the conference room. She headed back to her office after the meeting, not even stopping to wave or chat with her coworkers like she normally did.

*Cortez Wallace...*she hadn't seen or talked to him in eight years. The morning after his argument with Correll, Julia told him she was sick. After he'd left for the station, she packed her things, typed a letter of resignation and mailed it to WPDM. She made a hasty show of saying goodbye to her family; she didn't think her mother ever forgave her for leaving so abruptly. Anyway, Julia had said to hell with it and set off for Los Angeles, which was as far as she could get on limited cash and no job prospects on the horizon. She had a girlfriend out there and roomed with her for about five months. All the while, she was determined to make it—away from Cortez.

She'd snagged a copyediting position with Haven Network, the parent company of Outlook TV. Her dedication and diligence quickly made her a valued employee. She moved up so fast within the ranks that when Haven launched Outlook, Julia was pulled aboard. Snagging a position as producer was a dream, and Julia went on to produce many of its most popular shows. Now she'd made a name for herself all over L.A. and beyond.

Still, the name *Cortez Wallace* had the power to make her feel the same way she did on the night she'd overheard his brother say those terrible things about her. Those words made her feel unworthy and cheap. The last eight years proved she was anything but, even though she'd known that all along. Still, a part of her wanted to show the Wallace family just how far she had come. Moreover, she wanted Cortez to know it—she wouldn't allow herself to think he already did. And besides, deep down, a part of her still wanted to delight in the pleasure she'd always found in his arms. After experiencing that pleasure just once more, maybe—*maybe*—she could truly move on with her life and let him do the same.

Right, Julia. Easier said than done, an annoying voice told her. After all, this was Cortez Wallace—tall, caramel-skinned, dark-eyed, steel-bodied Cortez Wallace. Her eight years in L.A. weren't nearly enough to make her forget what a physical specimen he was.

"Forget it," Julia chided herself, raking her fingers through her short hair. What she needed to focus on was making it clear to Cortez that he'd just be reopening a can of worms by relocating and working with her in California. Maybe if her chauvinist colleagues couldn't get Cortez to sign, they'd forget the show completely. That way, Cortez would be back in Detroit where he belonged. He wouldn't be in such close proximity every second, easing his way back into her heart.

She hoped.

Chapter 2

"Ma, how many times do I have to tell you that article was inaccurate?"

"Cortez, shhh..."

Flashing Renee a murderous glare, Cortez fell silent and reclined in the chair he'd occupied for the past twenty minutes. Cora had insisted that he and Renee come out to her house for lunch. Cortez only agreed on the condition that he and Renee spend the time convincing Cora that she, and probably all of Detroit, had been misinformed.

Renee, however, hadn't lived up to her part of the bargain. She practically beamed as Cora went on and on about the engagement party she wanted to give them. Cortez massaged his eyes and silently chanted the phrase "calm down." He knew that once his mother was fixed on an idea, there was little that could dissuade her. Clearly, Renee was in no mood to do so.

"Ma, the article was a lie," Cortez stated bluntly, ignoring the quick glance Renee sent his way.

"Ah-hem," Cora grunted, reaching for her copy of the society section. "'We're both very *committed* to our *exclusive* relationship. We look forward to what's on the horizon,'" Cora recited Renee's statement, seemingly oblivious to Cortez's objections.

"Now, to me that doesn't sound like a misprint," Cora argued primly, folding her arms over the page as she looked down her nose at her youngest son. "Unless you're calling Renee a liar, dear?"

Cortez responded with a look that left no doubt that he was calling Renee just that. A moment later, Renee was excusing herself to the restroom. Cora scoffed at her son, who took little notice of Renee leaving the dining room.

Cortez recalled the relationships he'd had over the last eight years. He'd taken great care to ensure that his heart wasn't part of the deal. Every woman he brought to his bed was well aware of this. Now a woman with whom he'd never shared anything more than a few business dinners fancied herself his fiancée.

Cortez tuned back in to his mother, who was blaring his name.

"Why are you treating Renee as though she's done something wrong?" Cora demanded.

"Because she has and she knows it," he stated bluntly, leaning back in his chair as his mother gasped. *"Our relationship—"* he couldn't say it without grimacing *"—has* been about nothing but work." He grated sarcastically. "You're jumping down *my* throat over something that, for once, is not my fault."

"I can't believe you feel this way about her when she's so lovely," Cora chastised, her light brown face drawn taut with anger. "I can't believe Renee misjudged the situation this way. Obviously you didn't realize that you were dealing with a *lady* and not someone like Julia Kelly."

Cortez felt his heart jerk painfully in his chest at the sound of her name.

"The fact that you *lived* with her for four years should've been some hint about her character," Cora went on, standing from the table as though she were too heated to sit. "You've fooled around with all those silly girls over the last eight years because that's all you were used to with that Julia. Now Renee is tearing through that shallow wantonness to show you what it means to be loved by a *real* woman—a lady."

Cora was right. Living with Julia those four years had given him some hint to her character. More than *some*. She was the best thing he'd known. That is, until he woke up one morning to find her gone. Her leaving hit him like an anvil—he'd never seen it coming, and he'd never gotten past the damage it caused once it hit. He wouldn't acknowledge that her refusal to discuss marriage had anything to do with his family's treatment of her. He *couldn't* acknowledge the truth in that, either. Cortez clenched his fist in a vain attempt to rein in his emotions. He could feel the needles prickling his palm as he stood. "You and Renee enjoy the rest of your lunch," he said, ignoring his mother as she called to him on his way out the door.

"Hey, Julia, wait up!" Marisa Delon called. She smiled when her friend stopped and turned around. "Girl, I don't know how you do this." She sighed, falling in step next to Julia.

A confused look fell over Julia's face. She raised her eyes from the folder she had been studying.

Marisa rolled her eyes toward the ceiling. "Honey, do you ever plan on taking a vacation?"

Julia shook her head and smiled. "I don't have a reason to. My life is my work."

"Ha! How admirable," Marisa said, tossing her braids across her shoulder.

Julia caught the sarcasm in Marisa's words and shrugged. It was true: her life was her work. She had not had any type of personal life in years, it seemed. Not that the opposite sex didn't try to change that at every turn. The lovely thirty-four-year-old woman turned heads wherever she went. Tall and slender, her short, jet-black hair framed her face perfectly. She wore little, if any, makeup. Her extremely dark skin was so clear and smooth that no other enhancements were needed. Julia was well aware of her looks but simply was not interested in romance.

"Hey, Cathy." Marisa greeted the receptionist.

Cathy looked up from her filing. "Good morning, ladies. Your messages are on the desk."

"You wanna have lunch today?" Marisa asked, as they headed down the hall and into her office. She set the thick folder she was carrying on her desk.

"All right," Julia absently replied, scanning the pink messages in her hand. "What time?"

"I won't be free until around one. That okay?"

"Yup. I'll see you then," Julia promised, turning toward her office. In her rush, she knocked Marisa's folder to the floor.

"Ah, girl, don't worry about that," Marisa said, as she knelt to help Julia with the papers.

Julia's hand faltered over what appeared to be copy for a story. Attached to the paperwork was a picture, and Julia could not pull her eyes away from it. A face from her past smiled out at her from the 4 x 5 glossy. "What's this?" she asked Marisa, waving the picture in the air.

"Fine, huh?" Marisa said, noticing Julia's expression as she studied the photo.

"Extremely," Julia admitted. *How in Heaven's name could he possibly be even more gorgeous than he was eight years ago?* "His wife?" she asked, her voice breaking on the word when she took in the woman at his side.

Marisa leaned in to glance at the photo. "Not yet, but I'm sure she's hoping for it. According to that article they're quite the item: coanchors in Detroit, adoring fans, and she clearly states that they're in an *exclusive* relationship."

Julia only nodded.

"I wonder if he's told her about this L.A. thing?"

Julia's expression sharpened and Marisa reacted with a sheepish grin. "Sorry, but it's been all the talk. Word is they're trying to woo him out here."

"Is that right?" Julia inquired lightly, her eyes fixed once again on the clipping.

"Yes," Marisa said, her eyes narrowing. "I'm sure you'll be hearing about it soon. They want all their producers on their best behavior when and if he decides to visit the station."

Julia didn't tell her friend that this man was the reason she'd called her in L.A. at 3:00 a.m. eight years ago and begged for a place to stay until she got on her feet.

"Well listen, Marisa. I should start working. I'll, uh, talk to you later," she said, waving as she headed off.

Escaping to her office, Julia's mind threatened to explode with all the Cortez thoughts she'd tried to suppress over the last eight years.

She'd never wanted to leave him, especially in the way she did. *The way I just cut him off.* She knew he'd been furious. She was too much of a coward to face him when he'd come to her parents' house to look for her. She could hear the anger in his voice as he tried to speak calmly with them. It turned into an ugly scene, but Julia believed it would be best if they never saw one another again.

Now, however, he had another woman on his arm. It was killing her to see it, since that woman should have been her. It would have been her if she'd had the guts to stay and fight for him. *To hell with the rest of the Wallaces!* She should've stayed. She knew he loved her in spite of the lies his family and the rest of Detroit's jealous staid black social elite rambled about her. He'd probably not trust her as far as he could throw her now. And love? That love was surely long dead. *Or was it?* She wondered, thinking of the photo of Cortez and Renee Scales.

She didn't look like his type, she thought. Actually, she looked like a younger version of Cora Wallace. Julia shivered at the thought but recalled the saying that men usually married women like their mother.

"Oh, Corky, what's happened to you?" Julia sighed, an amused half smile on her lips. It might be interesting to see how serious this thing was, she debated. Knowing that he was truly committed to someone who loved him the way he deserved to be might be the one and only thing to rid her of the infatuation she still harbored for him.

In the circular drive outside his mother's house, Cortez slammed his hands to the hood of his Expedition and ordered himself to stay calm for what had to be the hundredth time that day. He'd tried with superhuman effort not to think of Julia Kelly. Ever. But hearing his mother speak her name was nearly his undoing, even after eight years. What really enraged him was the fact that his mother was right. The women over the last eight years had been a reaction to Julia, but not for the reasons Cora believed.

Julia had ravaged his thoughts after she left, to the point that Cortez could barely focus on a thing. His temper snapped at any and every thing. After a while, he accepted the fact that it was only a matter of time before he beat the living hell out of someone if they riled him up too much. Luckily, he had his job to fall back on. The job saved him, and he delved into it rigorously—making a well-known name for himself in the process. With that name and other irresistible attributes, women practically fell to his feet. He indulged, of course, believing that every moment spent in their arms was a moment he spent not being tortured by Julia. Sadly, *every* moment spent with another woman filled his thoughts of only Julia and the pleasure he'd found only with *her*.

Tiny chimes pierced the air and Cortez welcomed the interruption of his cell phone.

"Hi, I just wanted to remind you of the studio interview later this afternoon," Sara said as soon as he picked up. "Makeup's expecting you in an hour," she added.

Cortez checked his watch. "I'm on my way," he said, already settling into the driver's side of his charcoal-gray SUV. "Anything else?"

"Yeah. A James Sealy from L.A. called. Do you know what that's about? Because he was very secretive about what he wanted to discuss," Sara recalled. "Anyway, he seems determined to talk to you and wants you to call him at your earliest convenience."

Cortez made no comment. He'd spoken to James before and appreciated the man's discretion when he spoke with Sara. "I'll call him after this interview's taped," he told his assistant.

"Great!" Sara chirped. "See ya."

Cortez ended the call and tossed his cell phone onto the passenger seat, his handsome face suddenly pensive as he thought. L.A. could be the perfect place to disappear for a week. The phone chimed again and he saw Renee's name on the face plate.

Yes, he thought, L.A. would be the perfect place to disappear for a few weeks.

Chapter 3

Julia rolled her eyes as she set the receiver onto the cradle more firmly than necessary. *How long?* She wondered. How long could she pretend sweetness at these offers? She'd just received her third invite to the Haven Network's annual mixer. The event, held by Outlook's parent company, was actually a highly publicized soiree that boasted a who's who guest list of television and film celebrities alike. Also in great attendance were the network execs and employees who made the corporation the lucrative business that it was.

Of course, those who'd attended one or more of the mixers knew what really went on there. Insiders had dubbed the event "The Haven Orgy," since almost every guest who attended wound up losing their underwear at some point during the evening.

Julia always received at least four or five invites to the party before the word spread that she wasn't going and there was no point in asking her. Party number one she'd attended as a faithful new employee. After party number two, she decided that that would be her last.

Besides, she now had her eyes set on a bigger, more gorgeous fish than any who attended the Haven gathering.

Relaxed on her patio, several feet away from the splendid inground pool, she thought about seeing Cortez again. What would his reaction be to her? What would hers be to him?

Unwillingly, her thoughts turned to Renee Scales. Julia couldn't help but wonder again at how serious their relationship really was. A twinge of doubt settled in her stomach at the idea of interfering, but she cast it off quickly. The article didn't say they were married or engaged, so there.

Besides, she wasn't going to have him tied to her bed the moment he walked through her door. She'd just be her usual sweet, sexy self, and if he couldn't resist…well then, that would just be that.

"Did you find your room all right, Mr. Wallace?"

Cortez had settled in the back of the gray limo, having told the driver not to bother holding the door for him. He'd just checked into a posh Beverly Hills hotel courtesy of Outlook TV. "Thanks, Gary, everything was fine," he told the driver.

"Cool," the young man said as he whisked the sleek car out into the late evening traffic. "Nice, huh? The hotel?" he inquired, once they were moving along steadily.

"Yeah, not bad. Not bad at all," Cortez chuckled, smoothing the back of his hand across his whiskered cheek.

"That place really knows how to woo its up-and-coming celebrities," Gary raved, referring to the station.

"I haven't signed any papers yet, man," Cortez assured him with a shrug. "I am curious, though," he admitted.

Gary grinned. "Well if you're not, that's bound to change after tonight."

"Meaning?" Cortez asked, his deep brown eyes sparkling with humor.

"Well, you're on your way to the producer's house now, and these people don't play around when they make an offer. Hell, I almost wet my pants when I found out how much they were going to pay me just to drive the car."

Cortez's deep laughter rumbled from the backseat.

"Once you see the producer's place, you'll be having visions of digs like that dancing in your head," Gary predicted.

"So that's where we're headed now?" Cortez asked.

"Yes. You'll be having dinner there tonight. Wonder if the producer's assistant'll be there?" Gary said, as though he were asking himself. "She's somethin' else," he told Cortez, having caught his eye through the rearview mirror.

"A beauty, huh?"

"Hell, yes," Gary confirmed heartily.

From there, the conversation for the remainder of the trip focused on Gary's love life, or lack thereof. He was clearly smitten by this assistant and praised her beauty almost reverently before vowing that he was going to ask her out soon.

"So why haven't you already?" Cortez inquired, watching as Gary shrugged rather stiffly.

"She's just so damn gorgeous and successful, and I'm a white limo driver. I don't want my heart broken, know what I mean?"

Cortez's gaze narrowed in understanding and he sighed while leaning back to survey the palm tree-lined streets. "Yeah, Gary, I know exactly what you mean."

The producer's home was set in one of L.A.'s many exclusive neighborhoods. Cortez was stunned by the size and majesty of the white brick mansion that appeared to have been constructed right in the middle of an exotic jungle. Gargantuan palm trees and other leafy brush cascaded elegantly around the home. There was even a man-made pond several feet before the entrance. Colorful fish darted amidst its beautifully clear water. The place could have easily made the cover of *Architectural Digest* and *Better Homes and Gardens* simultaneously. The exquisite creation truly put his overpriced Beverly Hills hotel to shame.

Tugging on the cuff of his midnight blue shirt, Cortez thought that if Outlook paid its on-air talent as well as its executives, he might not be so quick to dismiss their offer once it was on the table. He rang the bell and waited, surveying the creative landscaping. The door opened and the strength left his legs before he even turned to see who had spoken.

"Good evening, Corky."

Cortez felt his eyebrows draw close and knew the furrow between them was etched deep. Leaning against the open door right before him and looking dangerously sexy was Julia Kelly. Cortez was unable to speak. Soon he, too, was leaning against the doorjamb as he searched the dark, lovely face before his very eyes as though it were some sort of apparition.

"Juli," he said finally, reaching out to curve his hand gently around her cheek before venturing upward to toy with her shortened hair. Finally, his hand rested around the base of her neck. His fingers massaged the silky column for proof that she was real.

The touch stirred up much emotion in Julia. Her lengthy eyelashes fluttered rapidly as a tiny moan escaped her mouth. Cortez's hypnotic chocolate stare focused on the lush curve of her lips and he jerked away as if she'd burned him.

"What the hell?" he breathed, shaking his head in wonder and irritation. "What the hell are you doing here?" he managed.

"You're having dinner with *me,* Corky."

Her matter-of-fact manner and the subtle heave of the bosom she knew he was struggling not to acknowledge roused his temper. "No, I'm having dinner with the producer," he corrected, rising to his full height.

Julia nodded once, seeing the captivation leave his eyes to be replaced by something stormier. "You're having lunch with my bosses tomorrow. Tonight, you're having dinner with me," she explained, folding her arms across the figure-flattering asymmetrical frock she wore.

Cortez didn't want to be affected by her, yet he wasn't surprised by his immediate response to her just the same. "I don't have time for games, Julia, and if I did I wouldn't fly halfway across the country to play them."

Julia threw her head back and laughed. She missed Cortez's murderous expression become a momentary helplessness as his eyes raked over the very-missed sight of her.

"Oh, Corky, I'm not playing games with you," she assured him at last, her ebony stare focused and alluring. "I prefer more satisfying ways to have fun," she whispered, her nostrils flaring when he leaned close and the incredible scent of his cologne drifted in the air.

"Good night," he told her, ignoring the obvious desire

in her eyes as she fixed him with a lingering look. "Tell the producer I'm sorry I misunderstood."

Julia blinked in sudden comprehension. "Cortez? Cortez, just who do you think I am?"

Realization dawned like sunlight on a hangover. He winced painfully as he realized his mistake. "You're the Outlook producer I'm having dinner with?"

"Bingo," Julia announced, before shaking her head. "Who'd you *think* I was? Besides, didn't the name Kelly ring a bell?"

Smoothing a large hand across his sleek, close-cut hair, Cortez grinned. "From the way the driver went on about what a dime the producer's assistant was..." he trailed off, taking in the chic short hairstyle that accentuated her incredible face.

Julia closed her eyes and nodded. "You must've had Gary. He's infatuated with my assistant, Lexi. We're all wondering when he'll get around to asking her out," she shared as the granite quality returned to Cortez's face. She offered a devilish smile in return. "Listen, I hope you're not as chauvinistic as my bosses, because clearly you expected to meet a man."

Cortez shrugged. "How chauvinistic can they be if you've risen to the rank of producer?"

Sighing in an overly dramatic fashion, Julia massaged her neck and grimaced. "That's a long and involved story that I really don't want to have on my front porch. Won't you please come inside?"

Cortez's warm gaze narrowed as it once again took in Julia's face and body. She had to be the only woman he'd ever met who could make a simple phrase sound like the most erotic sexual innuendo. Without another word, he stepped forward to accept her invite.

"Would you like a tour?" Julia called, noticing Cortez

looking around the interior of the home, which was designed just as exotically as its exterior.

"What am I doing here?" Cortez asked without turning to face her.

Julia's expression darkened. "The big boys want you to host their show," she drawled, strolling barefoot out of the entrance hall and down the glass steps leading to the living room. "Of course, the original idea was mine, and *of course* they twisted it into their own and figure only a man can make it work."

"And clearly you're not pleased by their logic," Cortez noted, stopping just inside the sunroom to watch her closely. "So why would they ask you to be part of my welcoming committee?"

Julia couldn't hide her uneasiness and put more distance between them. "They know I used to work with you at WPDM and figured we were old friends. They thought it might make the trip *easier,* for lack of a better word."

"I'm surprised you agreed," Cortez said, his deep voice soft and probing. "Considering the way we *left* things, for lack of a better word."

That was absolutely the last thing Julia wanted to discuss. Clearing her throat, she made a pretense of rearranging the throw pillows on the cream sofa cushions. "They agreed to make me coproducer on the show. I'll also be given the go-ahead to test my show once this one fails. Would you like a drink?" she offered, breezing deeper into the living room.

"Why would they predict the failure of a show they seem so eager for?" Cortez asked, reaching out to take the glass of Hennessey that Julia had provided.

"*They* aren't predicting its failure. *I* am. I thought your agent would've mentioned that."

Cortez nodded, recalling the conversation with his

agent, Perry Boykins. Several times, he'd gotten the idea that Perry was keeping something hidden. Now he realized the man probably didn't want Julia's involvement to make him pass on the deal of a lifetime.

Cortez enjoyed his drink while Julia relayed her show's premise. She was quite firm in her opinion as to why having a woman take on the challenges of the show would be far more interesting.

It was clear that she had a definite mastery of her job, but he was having trouble staying focused on the topic. Cortez was utterly taken by the woman who sauntered before him, speaking facts and figures while everything else about her shrieked sensuality and loveliness. She'd always been confident and alluring, but the assuredness that came with maturity and experience added something even more provocative to her persona. Cortez knew he was in trouble.

"So when's dinner?" he asked, cutting Julia off mid-sentence. Unfortunately, it was that or get out of that house as fast as his legs would carry him.

Julia smiled, before waving her hand lazily. "Just this way," she instructed, and led the way to the adjoining patio. It was set like a scene for seduction. Candlelight flickered invitingly, casting its savage beauty against the leafy palms, fichus and ferns that adorned the area. Cortez settled into the chair Julia held out for him.

"Be right back," she spoke close to the vicinity of his ear before leaving the room.

Cortez reminded himself to play it cool. She had to know what she was doing to him as she casually brought the meal to the table they were sharing. Propping his cheek to his fist, his smoky brown eyes followed her every move. Watching her walk back and forth, on her small bare feet, his thoughts drifted back to them together—together in heated, explicit detail. Those details flashed sharp and vivid due in no small part to the fact that the candlelight made the olive green material of her dress appear transparent.

"There, I think that's all," Julia breathed, tapping a rounded nail to her cheek as she observed the table. "Ah!" she called, moving over to reach a decanter. "Wine?" she offered, leaning across his shoulder to fill his glass with a deep red Chianti.

Smothering a frustrated sound, Cortez angled his athletic frame to give her extra room. Not to mention that her proximity was threatening to turn his semihard arousal to a more potent state.

"I'm sorry," Julia started, deliberately mistaking his tense actions. "Are you unhappy with the wine? Maybe you'd like something stronger?"

Cortez massaged the bridge of his nose. "No, thanks. I'm fine. Can we just eat?"

"Sure, Corky," Julia whispered as she prepared him a mouthwatering plate of homemade three-cheese manicotti. There was spinach salad, asparagus tips and plump, moist sourdough rolls to top off the meal. Julia remained silent for a while, wondering if he recalled that the dish had been her specialty when they lived together eight years ago.

"So, tell me about your job," Julia urged, after the silence began to feel too overwhelming. "Are you really ready to leave a place where you now wield so much power?"

Cortez shrugged, shaking more Parmesan onto his manicotti. "It depends. I guess I'll have to hear Outlook's offer first. They've already got me sold on the weather," he confided, focused on his food as he spoke. "I'll take this over a Detroit winter any day."

Julia tried not to appear overly confused. He didn't sound as though he'd miss Michigan much. Did that mean the woman in the photo really wasn't that special? Or did it mean that she'd be ready to relocate to L.A. with him? Deciding she wasn't ready to know, Julia changed the topic. They spoke about current events and the weather throughout the rest of their meal.

"Would you like dessert? I made an apple tart."

Cortez grinned and shook his head. "I won't be able to walk out of here if I do," he said, noticing the twinkle in Julia's eyes that said she wouldn't mind that at all. "I'd better be getting back to my hotel," he decided.

Julia checked the silver Rolex draping her wrist. "Gary won't be back for another forty-five minutes. How about that tour?" she offered, already standing.

Cortez shrugged and rose from the table, as well. Julia realized she was staring, taking in his facial features that the last eight years had helped to define as magnificently as the rest of him. He appeared far more cut than he had when they were together. What she wouldn't give to find out for herself…

Cortez cleared his throat and Julia snapped to. The lower-level portion of the tour was almost educational, with books, artwork and sculptures gracing every room. Vibrant, captivating paintings and towering bookcases filled with writing from every genre gave each room a personality of its own. Cortez verbalized his approval of the recreation room and library. Sadly, the easy feelings disappeared when Julia showed him the upper level of her home.

Cortez thought the trip upstairs would never end, with Julia's bottom in the direct line of his gaze and waging war on his hormones. She showed him around the spa and music room, complete with a fully stocked bar and dance floor. Then she gave him a quick look at the guest rooms.

"What's there?" Cortez inquired, with a slow wave toward another wing when he saw Julia was preparing to return downstairs.

Saying nothing, but wearing a decidedly smug smirk on her mouth, Julia headed toward the overlooked wing. The entire wing housed her bedroom suite. It was a room that practically blared "Enter only if you wish to be seduced."

Cortez took in every aspect without it even occurring to him how intently he was surveying it. Specifically, he was looking for a trace of anything other than *feminine* articles within the area. Why it mattered to him whether she allowed a man to share the dwelling was a thought he didn't want to entertain.

Once his private appraisal of the room had ended, he turned to find Julia lying on her stomach. She was propped on her elbows upon a magnificent bed.

"Isn't it great?" she teased, biting her lower lip as she wriggled a bit atop the gorgeous gold coverings. "I spent a few weeks in Jamaica last year, and these were the beds they had in the hotel," she explained. "I begged them to let me buy one, and I make the most out of every minute I spend in here."

"I'm sure," he commented, knowing her outrageous behavior was a ploy to see how far she could push him. True, Julia Kelly knew better than anyone how to push his buttons. So it was only fair now, he decided, to push a few of hers.

Julia moved to sit when Cortez strolled over to the bed's edge. She sat looking up at him with an expression that was half challenging and half wanton. Slowly, suggestively, her onyx stare drifted from his gorgeous caramel face, past his broad shoulders and chiseled chest. She was eye level with the leather belt around the black trousers on his lean waist.

"So…" she trailed off in a vaguely inviting manner.

"Know what I'd like to do?" Cortez asked, going down on his knees before her to give the impression that his motives were purely seductive.

Julia felt her mouth go dry as her lips parted. She couldn't think when he leaned close. Her own erotic intentions evaporated when she felt his breath on her skin. His nose was mere inches from her collarbone. Clenching the bed coverings was a feeble attempt to keep her from tugging him closer.

"What I'd really like to do…" he said, his nose grazing her jaw and then the sensitive area below her ear. "I'd really like to talk about eight years ago."

Spoken in the soft baritone of his voice, the words doused Julia in icy cold. Her expression tightened with hurt and surprise, but she quickly collected herself.

"Damn, would you look at that?" she whispered, glancing again at her watch. "Gary should be here any minute."

Smiling as though her reaction was expected, Cortez nodded and stood.

Julia buried her face in her hands when he left the room.

The executives for Outlook TV presented an impressive package to Cortez the next afternoon during lunch at Maze, a fancy seafood restaurant in downtown L.A. The group spoke not only about the show and their offer, but of retirement, health and stock options. By the time Julia arrived, Cortez had them all laughing about the fact that if he'd known he was such a hot ticket he'd have demanded a raise years ago.

"Oh, please," Julia instructed, waving a hand when every man at the table stood. Of course, she took her seat without offering the slightest apology for being late.

"We expected you some time ago, Julia."

"Well it obviously didn't stop you from eating, Ben," Julia remarked snidely to Bennett Daniels across the big, round table.

"You've got a lot riding on this guy, too, Julia," someone pointed out in a teasing voice.

Julia wasn't amused. "I suppose you're right. Since the sooner *he* starts, the sooner the show can flop and I can have my shot."

"Julia!

"What?" Julia retorted, with a flip shrug at James. "We're all friends here," she went on, picking invisible lint from her powder-blue pantsuit. "Cortez knows how I feel about this."

"Then at least pretend for our sakes, Julia," Kenrick urged.

Cortez enjoyed the scene. He reclined in his chair, awe-filled as he watched Julia and the way the table full of high-powered male executives practically begged for her cooperation. Suddenly he didn't feel quite so pathetic for having so little resistance in her presence.

"Well, we're all done with lunch," Bennett snapped.

"Fine, I've already eaten anyway," Julia said and grabbed her purse.

The group dispersed with Cortez heading off with Bennett and the other executives. James pulled Julia aside with him.

"Listen to me good, Julia," he began, leaning close. "Until Cortez Wallace signs on the dotted line, consider your coproducer title and the promise of this new show of yours to be up in the air."

Julia's eyes widened. "You can't."

"Oh, but I can."

"That's crazy! You can't let my show hinge on whether or not you can sell him on—"

"Nevertheless, Julia," James interrupted again, "that's the way it is—take it or leave it. But I suggest you start playing ball and get rid of the attitude."

Julia contemplated her options as she often did when James or any of the other executives tried to pull the power card. Those options were numerous and lucrative. Still, she'd come too far at Outlook TV to walk away from her position in a huff. Regardless of how far things had progressed, black women who'd amassed the sort of power she'd acquired were still too few and too far between. She knew how to play the game, but that didn't mean she couldn't be pissed about the rules.

Without another word, Julia stormed away from the table and knocked over a chair as she left. James shook his head at Cortez when their eyes met.

"Nothing's ever as good as it seems," James told Cortez. "Julia Kelly's tops in her field. Everybody wants her."

"In more ways than one," someone remarked, causing a soft rise of male laughter.

James continued, "She's intelligent, she's beautiful, she's complex and she treats men like we're dumb blondes only good for one thing. I think every man who meets her falls in love with her." He shook his head and motioned toward Cortez. "But you know her better than any of us here."

"And I couldn't have said it better myself," Cortez agreed, earning another round of laughter from his lunch mates.

Chapter 4

A day later, Cortez sat with his eyes narrowed, watching the candlelight reflect off the ice and Scotch in his glass. Julia sat with her chin resting in her palm, while her fingers tapped a slow, morose tune on the white tablecloth. In keeping with her "tour guide" duties, Julia decided to take Cortez out to one of her favorite restaurants. Unfortunately, the gorgeous environment did nothing to dispel the tension between them. At last, the silence became too much.

"The food here is great, but they take their sweet time in bringing it out," Julia remarked, casting a vapid look around the mellow dining area of Jazzy's Supperclub. "Would you like to dance?" she offered in a bright tone.

"No." Cortez declined without so much as a glance in her direction.

"Why? Is it against the rules? Are you not allowed?" Julia probed. Her expression was fixed and clear.

Swallowing what remained of his drink, Cortez stood. Julia gasped when he took her upper arm and led her to the glossy, pine dance floor.

"I didn't say that for you to have to try and prove anything, Corky," Julia said as they claimed their spot amidst the other slow dancers.

"Juli?" Cortez spoke sweetly, though the look he sent her was anything but. "Do me a favor and shut up," he said, his grip growing so tight that Julia gasped again.

Of course, her gasp was for a different reason this time. It felt as though every muscle of his torso was clearly defined against her body. She wondered if he could feel her nipples harden through the silky fabric of the magenta blouse she wore.

"Did I touch a nerve, Cortez?" she whispered then, blinking when his hand encircled her neck.

He tilted back her head so she could look directly into his eyes. "Why do you feel the need to push me?"

Julia had the nerve to smile. "It's just so much fun."

"Well just wait until you get what you're asking for and it's more than you expect. Or want," Cortez whispered into her ear.

"It could never be more than I want," Julia breathed in return.

Cortez grinned, sparking his dimple. She had absolutely no idea how dangerous it was to goad him. She wanted to sleep with him again, over the last week she made that very clear. Everything she did in his presence screamed it, and here he was denying himself a chance to reindulge in the best sex he'd ever had. But he knew if he did, he'd be hooked on her. He had never been able to rid himself of his love for her. He didn't know if he could recover if she ever walked away—again.

"So tell me about Detroit?" she asked casually, easing her hands up over his rust-colored shirt to link them behind his neck. "There must be someone special there."

Suspicious now, Cortez tilted his head just slightly closer. "Why would you ask that?"

"Corky, please! You're so on edge I can practically see the tension radiating off your shoulders," she observed, idly stroking the silky texture of his hair where it tapered at his neck. "You won't even let yourself relax around me for fear that you'll do something unforgivable." She arched farther into the rock solid expanse of his chest as they swayed to a suggestive sultry sax piece. "I think you're afraid that this—" she snuggled against the delicious stiffness pressing against the zipper of his cream trousers "—might end up in the wrong place." A phony look of shock brightened her eyes. "My, my, is that for me...or her?"

Cortez took hold of her bottom, trapping her in an unbreakable embrace. Since the floor teemed with lurid dancers, his actions went unnoticed. When his head dipped closer to her own, Julia felt her lips tingle and prayed he would kiss her.

"It looks like our food's finally here," he whispered, and left her standing on the dance floor.

"This really isn't necessary. You are the guest here. We should've dropped you off first." Julia decided to give it a rest. They were almost to her home. She'd been questioning his decision to drop her off first since they left the restaurant and he instructed Gary.

Cortez, however, didn't trust himself to head to his hotel. Julia might insist on seeing him inside and he doubted he'd let her leave until the sun was streaming through the windows. No, this was safer. Besides, he'd already promised himself a trip to the hotel bar to drown his frustrations, sexual and otherwise, in a bottle of burning whiskey.

"I got her, Gary." Cortez instructed the driver to remain where he was. He'd see Julia to the door.

Julia saw that they were rounding the steep horseshoe drive leading to her home. Smoothing both hands across her shimmering multicolored silk skirt, she breathed in deeply and waited for Cortez to open her door when the limo pulled to a halt. They walked to her front door in silence and Cortez waited while she unlocked it and strolled inside. He was turning to leave when her voice touched his ears.

"You should really do something about that lump in your pants. It's impressive, but you might give Gary the wrong idea," Julia called over her shoulder and smiled smugly as she delivered the parting shot.

A second later Cortez was right behind her, all six-feet-plus, caramel-toned muscular inches of him. Her keys spilled to the floor, their clatter mingling with the rush of heavy breathing and smothered moans. Her purse followed, the contents littering the marble floor. Cortez held her pinned against the marble message table, the only furnishing in the spacious foyer. They were facing the large mirror above it. Julia's strappy gold heels clicked upon the floor as Cortez forced her legs apart and he eased a massive thigh between.

Julia gasped at the determination on his handsome face. He tugged up the hem of her skirt and ripped away her panties without a second thought. She closed her eyes and pressed her lips together when his perfect teeth gnawed at her neck. His fingers had begun a persuasive assault by teasing the satiny flesh of her inner thigh. Julia wanted to slide to the floor when his thumb manipulated the extra-sensitive flesh guarding her womanhood. He wouldn't allow her to escape him and leaned in, pressing her closer to the imposing desk.

Julia's wavering moans echoed in the high ceiling foyer when Cortez added his index finger to the fondling session. It ventured deep, forcing a trembling cry from Julia's mouth. She began to move up and down over his thrusting finger, tugging her lower lip between her teeth as she gave the act her complete concentration.

Cortez felt a flood of creamy moisture drench his skin when his middle finger alternated between dipping and rotating inside her walls.

Julia couldn't move, not that she wanted to. Being virtually immobile made the pleasure even more enjoyable. Her head fell back against his shoulder and she studied him as he focused and concentrated on pleasuring her. She moaned unashamedly and in desperate need for him to continue.

Cortez had wanted to punish her for teasing him to the point of no return but he hadn't meant to enjoy this so much. Each thrust of his fingers as he curved them deeper sent his arousal soaring. Julia muttered something incomprehensible when he pulled her back onto his engorged sex. Her fingers were splayed across the mirror and her forehead was pressed against the cool glass.

Julia realized she had one question answered. No man's touch could equal his. In eight years she'd never become orgasmic by a man simply making love to her with his fingers. But there she stood, panties ripped and lying on the floor of her foyer while this man whom she hadn't spoken to in almost a decade ruled her body and her desires with his touch.

Her gasping cries ebbed as the power of a massive climax began its ascent. She lost control of her reasoning as she spread her legs farther apart to offer him more room to play.

The hand that had been gripping Julia's hip rose to close around her throat. He made her look at him in the mirror. "Why did you leave me?" he asked.

Julia's stomach tightened and she could scarcely think. "Cortez, please don't," she begged, now for a totally different reason. The thrusting that drove her mad slowed to a snail's pace, which made the act far more torturous.

"Don't I deserve to know?" His soft voice sounded harsh and hollow.

"Mmm," Julia moaned, closing her eyes against the sight of his gorgeous face reflected in the mirror.

"Juli?" he taunted, alternating the sensual lunges between his index and middle fingers.

"Oh, Cortez, please, it's in the past," she groaned. "Mmm," she moaned again as she contracted around both of the fingers that were now inside her.

Cortez flexed his hand slightly around her neck, the thrusts turning rapid once more. Julia shrieked her approval, urging him on with soft whispers of, "Yes, that's it, that's it…"

"Tell me, Juli," he insisted.

She winced, irritated in the midst of pleasure. "Damn it, can't you please just let this go?" she snapped.

His eyes narrowed and he played with her only a few seconds more before suddenly depriving her of his touch.

"Yeah…yeah, Juli. I can let it go," he said, smirking as he watched her shudder and hold on to the desk for support. He collected the black satin panties from the floor and used them to wipe her moisture from his fingers.

"You know where I am when you're ready to tell me why," he said, and left without a backwards glance.

"This is out of the question. You guys are going too far now!"

"Calm down, Julia," Bennett urged.

"Hell, at least lower your voice," James proffered.

Julia raked her fingers through her short hair and took several deep breaths. "This has got to be against some sort of harassment rules or something," she noted, turning to face him. "You can't *make* me go out with this man to get him to accept a job."

"Well, Julia, of course you don't *have* to agree to this."

Pursing her lips, Julia folded her arms across the front of her crisp, pin-striped shirt.

"Look, Julia, we simply want Cortez to see every aspect of the company," Ben reasoned. "Attending the Haven party—"

"Orgy," Julia corrected.

"Mixer," Ben rephrased, "will show him that we're a fun, laid-back group that encourages creative expression and welcomes input from all employees."

"In short, we just think it'll impress the hell out of him," James said.

"Then what do you need *me* there for?" Julia demanded, tugging at her shirt's stylish, quarter-length cuffed sleeves.

James went to fix himself a drink. "Because he wants you there. He told us what a great time he had at dinner last night."

"Yeah, he said if everyone here was as fantastic as you, he might very well consider a change," Ben added.

"Well then give him a chance to find out. Fix him up

with one of the other women here," Julia suggested, not caring whether Ben and James noticed the desperation in her voice. "They're all dying to get to know him," *and have their panties ripped off after dinner,* she thought silently.

It had been a mistake to prod and tease Cortez, she should have known that. She'd been in control until he'd asked that. The determination in his eyes told her that he wouldn't stop until she told him, forcing her to relive the only time in her life she'd truly felt ashamed.

Still, as much as she hated his family, she didn't want to be responsible for *him* hating them. He was sure to, if she told him they were the reason she put an end to their future. Worse, she could tell him and he'd wind up hating her. Well...hating her more than he did now.

"Julia? Jules, you with us?"

Snapping to, Julia offered a quick smile.

"Can we count on you?" Ben asked.

"Fine," she said and left the office.

The soothing, heavy spray of water sleeked and beaded across Cortez's toned, athletic frame as he stood beneath the showerhead that morning. Last night he'd helped himself to a few glasses of Jim Beam and celebrated doing what he was sure few men could've, or *would've,* done in a similar situation. He'd gone to bed semihard and awakened firm and erect with images of Julia Kelly flooding his dreams. Holding all that dark sensuality in his arms was tantamount to Heaven. Of course, sex was just the incredible payoff for what he was really after.

Being with her again, having her back in his life was what he wanted. But it could never be. He wouldn't allow it. Losing her was unexpected and it had nearly shut him down. It scared the hell out of him to think about what it would do to him now. Her leaving again would be the end of him. He'd said that before, and the fact grew more credible with each day he spent in her presence.

He shut off the water and dried off, but his thoughts remained heavy. In the bedroom he saw the invite to the Haven party lying on the dresser. From conversations during the meetings he'd attended, it was clear that the event was not to be missed. He was more than a little curious about what was in store.

Julia ran across his mind again. He'd requested her as his escort at first just to wreak havoc on her emotions, but soon it was about more than just that. He'd be leaving for Detroit the day after the party, and he at least needed to know why she left, why she didn't trust him enough to let him face it with her. Then he could move on and leave her in the past, hopefully. He swore she'd tell him if he had to use every trick he knew to get the answers he'd waited for too long to hear.

Julia spent a lazy afternoon in a bikini while relaxing by the pool. She decided to give her sister a call before heading upstairs to prepare for the Haven soiree.

"I wonder why he hasn't told me about her?"

Monique Kelly laughed. "Well, with the way you've been throwing yourself at him, he probably figures on one last fling before the big day and doesn't want to mess up a sure thing."

Julia rolled her eyes at her older sister's perspective. She groaned when the woman's laughter gained volume as it fluttered through the phone receiver.

"Do you think it's that serious?" Julia couldn't help but ask, as a look of unease settled within her dark eyes.

From her home office in Detroit, Monique reclined in her desk chair and surveyed her view of downtown.

"It seems to be, little sis," she admitted, hearing the full silence on the other end of the line, "but you of all people know how the media can blow things out of proportion."

The tiniest pool of hope sprang someplace deep in Julia's heart. It evaporated at Monique's next statement.

"It *is* a perfect match, though. Coanchors on the same show, a town full of fans, well-wishers and all that jazz. Besides, I'm sure Cora just loves her."

"All right, Mo, I get it. You've made your point," Julia noted morosely.

"Forget him, Jukee," Monique warned her sister.

"But I thought you always liked Cortez?"

"I *did,* but his family made you feel like dirt and it affected you for the worse. Being in L.A., accomplishing what you have, don't toss it all away for something as uncertain as love," Monique preached.

Julia couldn't argue. She knew that her sister had a very good reason to be cynical in light of her own past experiences. "I hear you, Mo," she said finally.

"Do you really?"

"I swear," Julia said just as the doorbell sounded. She practically repeated Monique's advisements word for word while strolling to the front of the house. But her affirmations trailed to silence as she opened the door to greet Cortez.

A grin brightened his handsome face, but he didn't appear amused. Instead, it seemed as though he wasn't surprised to find her answering the door wearing a bikini. Still, that didn't stop him from appraising the appealing vision she cast.

His entrancing brown eyes raked over her slender dark chocolate frame encased in a white string bikini trimmed in hot pink. His gaze locked onto the small heart cut into the material of the bikini top. Slowly, she turned to speak into the phone she held and he saw an identical heart cut into the bottom, which allowed a glimpse of satiny ebony skin amidst a sea of white.

"I'll call you back later," Julia told Monique and clicked off the phone.

"Don't tell me, you were talking and just lost track of the time," Cortez guessed sarcastically.

"Exactly," Julia replied in an airy voice and whisked out of the foyer and toward the living room. "Would you like a drink before I go up to get dressed?" she offered, her body growing warm when she felt him behind her. She was still determined to show him that he didn't have the upper hand. Her skin riddled with gooseflesh, she turned to fix him with a bold look.

Cortez braced one hand against the long, brass bar cart behind her. The other rose to skirt her waist, his thumb brushing the tiny belly ring she sported, before fiddling with the ties that secured the bikini bottom at her hips. His intensely focused eyes searched hers for any sign of weakness.

"This is nice," he complimented softly, tracing her skin that showed through the heart cut into the bottom. "Is it your way of telling me you want more of what you got last night?" he inquired, now cupping one breast and circling his thumb around a firming nipple.

"I should be asking if you're trying to tell *me* that you want more of what *you* got last night," Julia countered, willing her eyelids not to flutter in response to his pleasurable attentions.

"Not so much fun being teased, is it?" he asked, now weighing her breast and squeezing her nipple between his thumb and forefinger.

A needy sound accidentally escaped her throat and

triumph gleamed on his face. "Teasing makes the follow-through more exciting. Only...you didn't follow through," she teased back seductively.

Cortez replied with a look of phony concern. "Disappointed?"

"Tsk, tsk." Julia gestured, her eyes narrowing as she smoothed her finger across his muscular forearm, bared by the short sleeves of the beige shirt he wore. "Again, Corky, I should be asking *you* that." Satisfied by her resistance, but knowing it was wearing thin, she sauntered across the room to the stairway. Turning the screw just a notch tighter, she pulled away the bikini top as she disappeared at the top of the stairs.

Cortez dragged his hand across his face and groaned. Then he turned to the bar and half filled a glass with cognac. Every nerve ending and hormone he possessed demanded that he take what she offered, what he'd wanted since he'd arrived on her doorstep over a week earlier. She was more determined to keep her secrets about eight years ago than he'd first realized. She was playing terribly unfair, using every single seductive, overpowering ounce of feminine allure to reel him in, and he was putting up no fight at all.

But then what? Then she'd be here in L.A. and he'd be on his way back to Detroit and hooked on her all over again. *Hell, man, when were you ever* not *hooked on her?*

Cortez splashed a bit more cognac into his glass.

"She's the only woman here who could snap her fingers and get any man in the place to drop his pants. That goes for the newest mailroom guy to the damn network president."

Cortez chuckled at the summation by Fred Chastwick, the Haven Network's VP of marketing and research.

"It's no joke," Fred assured, smoothing a hand across his bald, dark head. "She's tops in her field, which makes her even more desired. Unfortunately, she's also very discriminating."

"And that's a bad thing?" Cortez inquired, slipping a hand into the side pocket of his mocha trousers.

Thomas Grant, Haven's sales VP, spoke up. "It's not a bad thing, but that *desirability* of hers makes lots of people believe she's gotten where she is by sleeping her way to the top."

Cortez studied the ice circling his glass. "And that's not true?" he probed, looking up to see the executives shaking their heads.

"She's smart," Thomas said, "she's determined, she's gorgeous and she's sexy as hell. In spite of a few jealous colleagues, she's respected, and in this town that's gold."

The story remained unchanged throughout the evening. Men and women alike had the best things to say about Julia. Cortez couldn't say he was at all surprised. He'd always known she'd go far. She should've made anchor long before him. She would have if she'd wanted it. But, as she often said, behind the scenes was where the real power resided. Unfortunately for him, she'd wanted that power more than she'd wanted a relationship with him. Or so he had believed. What did surprise him was the discovery that she was so unattainable. That part had him intrigued. Julia Kelly wore her sensuality on her sleeve. She had to be aware of how desired she was. Why the ice-princess routine?

After three hours, Julia was more than ready to leave the Haven mixer. She'd already walked in on several couples making out in various areas of the mansion. Of course, no one had the decency to stop when they realized their privacy had been interrupted.

The party, held at the Beverly Hills estate of Haven's president, called for casual attire, which ranged from shorts and T-shirts to bathing suits and string bikinis. Julia opted for a lovely black one-piece suit that drew her several stares but was rather conservative for her personal tastes.

Even Gary, the chauffer, had finally decided to get over his shyness and make his move on Julia's assistant, Lexi Smith. Walking in on the two of them *enjoying* one another, on the balcony outside the ballroom, was about all Julia could stomach. She had no idea where Cortez had disappeared to and felt it best that she not go looking. Instead, she decided to wait for Gary at the car. She took solace in the quiet darkness at the rear of the limo and had almost a half hour of silence before the driver's-side door opened.

Cortez looked inside. Apparently he was searching for Gary, as well, when he caught sight of Julia in the back of the plush vehicle.

"Damn, you had me worried," he scolded, his frown deepening.

"Worried or jealous, Cork?" she taunted, toying with the fringed hemline of the wrap skirt she wore around her swimsuit. "Clearly my hideout isn't that good," she sighed while he remained silent.

"I was going to ask Gary about you," he admitted, still watching her from the driver's side.

Julia almost broke into laughter. "Honey, Gary is in Heaven right about now."

Cortez closed his eyes, a grin sparking the lone dimple

he possessed. Needing no further clarification, he closed the door and came around to join her in the back.

"So, is all this too much for you?" he asked, once he was relaxing next to her on the long backseat.

Julia shrugged. "It always is. That's why I never attend."

"So why are you here tonight?"

"Because of you. They said you requested me."

Cortez gave a quick shake of his head. "So what? From what I hear you call your own shots."

Julia rested her head upon the black cushioned back of the seat. "They begged me to be a team player. They want you *very* much."

"And what about you?" Cortez asked, the soft depth of his voice adding more potency to the words.

Julia didn't pretend to misunderstand them. She felt her thighs weaken in response. "That depends." She told him.

"On?"

"On whether you're available for the wanting," she clarified, turning to judge his reaction.

Cortez had been watching her steadily. When her eyes met his, he forgot all his warnings to stay away and pulled her across the seat to him. Julia's nails raked his stubble-roughened jaw just as his mouth crashed down upon her own. The kiss was forceful but it was also rather coaxing, slow and sultry. His tongue thrust leisurely, drawing low moans from her throat. Julia tried to chant his name, but her voice was effectively muffled beneath his kiss. She responded instead by kissing him back just as sweetly, just as seductively.

The tenderness he showed proved to be every bit as devastating as his commanding power over her body.

Cortez unfastened the straps of her bathing suit easily, his lips slowly encircling the circumference of one breast.

"Mmm…" Julia gestured weakly, arching her back to draw his focus to an aching nipple. "Cortez, plea—" her words broke when he satisfied her request and raked his teeth across the rigid bud. Julia let her hands fall from his gorgeous face, and she arched herself deeper into his mouth. Now Cortez was cupping both mounds, alternating licking and nibbling as he lost himself in her curves.

Hushed words of desire swirled within the dark confines of the car. Cortez uttered soft, tortured moans as he suckled Julia's nipples eagerly. His fingers skirted her rib cage and abdomen before disappearing beneath the hem of her wrap skirt. Julia tried to unfasten the buttons along the casual cotton shirt he wore. Her hands ached to caress the chiseled expanse of his broad chest. Cortez wouldn't allow it and took her wrists in his broad grip, trapping them above her head. His touch beneath her skirt grew bolder. His sensuous lips feasted on her bosom while his fingers sought and discovered the treasure they yearned for.

Julia cried out in pleasure when she felt him enter her body. His middle finger curved inside her and slowly increased the penetration. "Cortez, please, please…I need more—"

"Tell me why you left," he commanded suddenly, unexpectedly.

Julia shuddered as much from his incredible touch as she did from his whispered request.

"Tell me," he spoke again, showering her breasts with brief satiny kisses before he looked up at her.

"Because I was afraid!" she admitted hotly.

Cortez frowned. "Afraid? Afraid of me?"

Julia forced herself not to look away. "Afraid that you'd

start to feel about me the same way your family did if I stayed."

"Julia—"

"I heard you talking to Correll, that night after we came back from dinner to celebrate your anchor position," Julia confessed, weary of denying him the explanation he deserved. "He was right, Cork," she insisted when his expression darkened. "It would've been too much pressure on you and your new career. People like your mother, they would've made it impossible for us to be together. Your career would've been less about your work for the station and more about your relationship with a girl from the wrong society branch and—"

"Damn it, Juli, I never cared about that!" Cortez hissed, pulling up to glare down at her.

"That's because you couldn't," she told him in a sad voice. "Cortez, the crap I took from your family was one thing, but hearing them say it to you... I didn't want you dealing with that. *I* didn't want to deal with it, and it would've only been a matter of time before it started to affect us. You have to know that."

Cortez moved to the other end of the long suede seat and kept his face averted while Julia fixed her swimsuit. She risked infrequent glances at his magnificent profile, her heart racing in preparation for his hate-filled rebuke.

That rebuke never came. Instead, a look of hurt and disappointment flashed in the soulful warm depths of his brown eyes.

"Do you know what you did to me when you left?" he asked rhetorically. "I loved you, Juli, and Heaven help me, I still do."

Julia reached out for him. "Cortez—"

"But I'll be damned if I let you in again just to lose

you," he said, ignoring the hand she extended. "I couldn't take that ever again."

Julia was speechless and watched as he left the car, appearing as though he'd told her far more than he'd intended. He said he could never let her inside again for fear that she'd leave him. How could she make him see that she never wanted to leave him again?

She realized then that she was still as in love with him as she had been eight years ago.

Chapter 5

Julia arrived late the next morning for the meeting at the station. She wasn't in the best mood and wondered why in the world James and Ben would call a meeting the morning after one of the Haven gatherings.

"Sorry, sorry," she apologized as she breezed into James's office suite. Her heart lurched when she saw that Cortez was already there seated at the round table where the other executives had gathered.

"It's all right, Julia, we haven't gotten started yet," Ben was saying as he prepared coffee for himself at the cart of breakfast goods they'd ordered from the cafeteria.

Julia barely registered Ben's words, she was so unnerved by Cortez's presence. After last night, she wanted to crawl into a hole and disappear. Hearing him bare his soul to her told her just how much she'd hurt him when she left. The knowledge of the blow she'd dealt to his heart wasn't an easy reality to stomach.

"Can we talk?" Cortez leaned forward and asked once she'd set her purse and portfolio next to her chair.

Various conversations mingled throughout the room. Clearly the meeting wouldn't be starting for quite some time. Julia barely made eye contact with Cortez as she nodded.

Nervous, she kept smoothing her hands across the chic navy dress that hugged her every curve. Cortez ordered himself to stop imagining that those were *his* hands roaming her body. Clearing his throat, he forced a stern gaze to her face.

"I asked everyone to meet with me this morning," he told her once they'd found a corner to huddle in.

Julia shook her head once. "Is something wrong?"

"I'm turning down the job."

"Why? Cor—"

"Juli, I think we both know why. You know I can't work here, with you."

"Cortez, that's silly. Do you know what they're prepared to offer you? Any anchor would kill for this position."

Cortez grinned, his warm stare narrowed adoringly. "Love, you don't have to sell me. I know what I'm giving up."

"Then why—"

"Because I can't work with *you*. It'd be too much, and you know that."

Julia didn't try to hide the pleading intensity in her dark eyes. "It wouldn't have to be that way."

He stepped closer, unable to resist curving his hand around the base of her throat as his thumb stroked her chin. "Now who's being silly? You know I have to go. My life is there. It's where I belong."

Julia folded her arms across her chest. "So I guess that

answers my question. There *is* someone back in Detroit. Someone you're very serious about."

Cortez blinked as though debating whether to confirm or deny the statement. "That's not why I'm saying this. You know that."

Julia realized he never said she was wrong about the "someone serious" back in Detroit. *Damn it, girl, do you need him to beat it into your head? He's not going to give up a devoted woman to traipse off with you not knowing whether you'll up and leave him again.*

"Cortez, I love you," she blurted, abandoning all pretenses of strength and coolness. "I was wrong to leave then, I admit that. I should've stayed and fought, but please…you can't punish me forever for making that mistake. Not when you know I'd give anything to have you back."

"Shh…" he urged, shaking his head. "You wouldn't even be thinking like this if I hadn't come here. This thing between us needs to stay in the past. It's where we need to keep it, for both our sakes."

"Cortez."

"I won't change my mind, Juli, and you shouldn't want me to," he advised, leaning close to brush his mouth across her cheek. "You've got a great life here, and I have one waiting for me back in Detroit."

"Corky, please," she whispered, tears streaming from beneath her lashes when she squeezed her eyes shut.

"Shh…" he soothed again, brushing away her tears with his thumbs.

"But why?" Julia asked, swallowing another sob as she stared up at him with a challenging expression. "I know you want me, and you say you still love me. Why—"

"Because you scare me!" he whispered in a fierce tone, and then muttered a curse at the admission. "I told you,

I won't take you again just to lose you. It'd be too much, Julia. I couldn't survive it."

She knew there was nothing she could say then that would change his mind. She needed more time to convince him, she decided. If only he'd said that he hated her, that she sickened him, even. He hadn't said those things. He said he loved her, but he was afraid. She was afraid, too. She was afraid that if she didn't do everything in her power to change where things stood, she'd lose the only man she'd ever loved forever.

Julia watched Cortez reclaim his seat at the round conference table and smiled. James, Ben and the rest of the group were about to be greatly disappointed. She'd reassure them, though. She was about to leave for Detroit, as well, and she'd return with Cortez's acceptance of the Outlook offer and a great deal more.

Chapter 6

"This is your captain. We are now approaching Detroit and will be making our landing in twenty minutes. We hope your flight has been enjoyable, and we thank you for choosing to fly with us."

Julia leaned back in her seat and focused her dark gaze outside the window. Twenty minutes, she thought, twenty minutes and she would be back home.

"Good morning, this is Cortez Wallace. Our top story this hour…"

The instant Julia heard his voice, her gaze snapped from the fantastic view of the clouds. The overhead television had been tuned in to Detroit news channel WPDM. When she saw him, Julia knew she would never love another man as long as she lived. She'd do whatever it took to have him again.

"Thanks, Cortez. Good morning, Detroit, I'm Renee Scales and…"

When the camera cut to Renee, Julia sat a little straighter in her seat. Her eyes traced the face staring back at her from the TV screen. The beginnings of a small scowl appeared on Julia's face. She watched the woman gaze adoringly at Cortez, when he turned to her.

Even Julia could not deny that Renee Scales was a beautiful woman. Her complexion was very clear, almost glowing. Of course, that could have been the work of a makeup artist, Julia thought. No matter how lovely Renee was, though, Julia could only think of the way Cortez responded to her in L.A. Was that the sign of a man hungry for exquisite passion or simply a man who wanted one last fling before the knot was tied?

Dismissing the couple on screen, Julia leaned back against the cushioned headrest. If their time together in L.A. told her one thing, it was that Cortez had learned to protect his heart very well, but he wore his desires on his sleeve. He wanted her as much as she wanted him. Still, she'd hurt him terribly and he'd never seen it coming. His heart and his ego had been irrevocably wounded and it would take a miracle to reach him past all that hurt. Taking a deep breath, Julia opened her eyes and looked at the television screen. Did she actually have the nerve or, in her opinion, the poor taste to cause friction between the couple? Love made a person to all sorts of things, from the truly outrageous to the most heinous. She knew deep down that there was a fine line she would never cross to win Cortez's love. Still, she had to be sure. She had to know if this was real. Her every instinct told her there was nothing between the two, but that was secondary. What mattered most was whether Cortez had once and for all closed his heart to her. Surely she could determine that without doing anything…improper.

* * *

"Thanks for joining us this hour. Tune in at noon for an update on today's top stories."

"And cut!"

Cortez and Renee sighed in unison. As they removed the microphones from their clothing they didn't notice the crew approaching the desk.

"Surprise!"

Cortez's and Renee's expressions were direct opposites. Cortez appeared irritated and sullen. Renee's face was glowing with happiness. The crew had organized a surprise party, bringing the studio to life with laughter and conversation.

"When did you guys do all this?" Renee asked, her light brown eyes darting from face to face.

"That's our secret, and it looks like we kept it well." Carlton Giles, one of the cameramen, spoke up. "We know you guys haven't broken the news yet, but, well...we just wanted to get a jump on all the other well-wishers."

Could this get any worse? Cortez asked himself while pushing his tall, lean frame out of the swivel chair behind the news desk. "You handle this," he told Renee when their eyes met.

Brightly colored bags and wrapped presents cluttered the desktop. When Cortez began to make his way out of the studio, several people urged him to stay and get over his shyness. Thankfully, the switchboard paged him and he celebrated the interruption.

"I mean it," he told Renee on his way past her.

Frowning, Renee grabbed his arm. "Don't forget our noon broadcast, sweetie," she said, and kissed his cheek to the delight of the group in the studio.

* * *

"Monique!" Julia screamed, when she spotted her sister in the airport lobby.

"Jukee!" Monique called, racing forward to grab her little sister in a bear hug.

Sighing, Julia hoisted the strap of her carry-on bag over her shoulder. "Girl, I'm so glad you came and not Ma."

Monique brushed the tendrils of her soft hair away from her face and nodded. "I understand, but she just cares. Like we all do."

"I appreciate it, Mo, but I love him," Julia whispered, her expression apprehensive.

"Is this all you have?" Monique asked, eyeing the five pieces of luggage surrounding her sister.

Julia smiled at her sister's sarcasm. In minutes they had collected the bags and were headed out of the airport.

"Honey, are you sure you want to do this? I mean, I haven't seen Cortez in a while, but on TV he looks very happy with his fiancée."

"You shouldn't believe everything you see on TV," Julia instantly replied, following her sister across the parking deck.

They reached Monique's car and dropped the luggage to the ground. "Girl, do you really expect him to dump the woman the minute he sees you?" Monique asked as she opened the trunk.

Julia helped her sister situate the bags in the back. "I don't expect him to, but he'll think twice about marrying her. *If* he's even thinking of marriage at all, which I really don't believe he is."

"You sure of that?"

The easy expression Julia had worn practically since embarking upon the Detroit trip began to fade. Her sister's challenging question turned Julia's easy look to one that was far more questioning. Slowly, almost dazedly, she leaned against the trunk of the car. Monique pressed her lips together and chose to remain silent. She didn't want to push, and from the look on her little sister's face, she didn't need to. It relieved her to see that Julia wasn't as overconfident as she appeared. That aspect of the woman's personality had gotten her in trouble more times than Monique could count.

"That story is most likely false. Society pieces can't always be taken at face value. Living in L.A., I know." Julia managed a weak yet refreshing smile for her sister. "Still, there's always the possibility…"

"That it could be true?" Monique supplied.

Julia nodded, smoothing her hands over her arms, suddenly chilly beneath the tailored tan shirt she wore. In her mind she was seeing the photo of Cortez and Renee Scales that had fallen from Marisa Delon's folder.

Monique turned to lean against the trunk then, too. "So I have to ask if you're willing to risk it. Your pride, dignity…to find out for sure?"

Julia stiffened. "Cortez loved me before I left all those years ago."

"The operative word there is *left*." Monique cleared her throat when she noticed Julia's gaze falter. "Maybe the *interest* he showed out in Cali was more about him trying to find out the reasons you left, reasons you would never share with him." Monique stood then and fixed her sister with a pointed look. "A man like Cortez Wallace… I'm sure he's got lots of tools to help him get the answers he wants."

Stroking shaky fingers through her hair, Julia looked up at Monique. "Seems you're right about that, since he definitely got his answers. I told him what I overheard that night eight years ago," she explained when her sister's jaw dropped.

"What did he say?" Monique's voice was close to a whisper as she gripped the trunk door.

"He told me I scared him." Julia would've laughed at Monique's stunned expression had she not been so preoccupied by the memory. "He said he couldn't survive taking me back just to lose me." Julia stood then and closed the trunk. "Does that sound like a man on the brink of marrying another woman?"

Monique watched Julia round the car and take her place in the front. Silently, she admitted she had no response to refute her sister's assumptions.

"Lil' girl, you better get in here and hug me!" Tamara Kelly ordered as soon as Julia stepped inside the house.

Julia had expected her mother to start in on her as soon as she walked through the door. Seeing the bright smile on the woman's lovely, dark face relieved her. "Mommy," she whispered.

"Baby," Tamara whispered, pressing a kiss to Julia's short, glossy hair. "I'm so glad to have you home," she told her daughter, pulling back to have a look at her.

"Thanks, Ma."

Tamara sighed and brushed a speck of lint from Julia's shoulder. "I guess it'd be another few months before you came home if Cortez wasn't practically engaged."

Julia rolled her eyes and stepped away from her mother. "Mommy, I don't need to hear this now. The plane ride was long and the snacks were *not* satisfying."

"Okay, okay. I'm sorry, honey. Let's get you something to eat," Tamara said, hustling her youngest daughter into the kitchen.

***

Julia lifted another forkful of chicken salad to her lips. "I can't believe they're separated after all this time," she solemnly noted, when her mother had informed her that her aunt and uncle were about to divorce.

Tamara refilled Julia's tea glass and took a seat next to Monique at the dinette table.

"Yeah, I guess they finally decided to stop lying to themselves that the marriage was worth holding on to."

Julia glanced at Monique, before she looked at her mother. "Are you trying to tell me something?"

Tamara regarded Julia with an innocent stare. "Excuse me?"

"Mommy…"

"Baby, I just wish you'd look at the situation with Cortez. He's probably getting married, for goodness' sake."

"He didn't speak of her once while he was in L.A."

"So? What difference does that make?"

Julia slammed her hands to the table and stood. "If he loved her he would've talked about her. He would've at least told me he was off limits, but he never did."

"Jukee, it looks like he's marrying the woman. Besides, he's a man, and men do tend to hide the fact that there's a little woman at home when they have a chance to make a…*connection* with another one," Monique tried to reason.

"I can't believe that. Cortez never struck me as that sort of man who'd humiliate a woman that way."

Monique and Tamara exchanged glances before they stood, too.

"Listen, girl, you're smarter than this and you know it. Cortez Wallace is not worth all that you're putting yourself through."

Julia rolled her eyes toward her mother but did not respond.

"I don't know why you want to be part of that family anyway," Tamara grumbled, as she cleared away the lunch dishes. "Cora Wallace ain't nothin' but an uppity old bitch."

Julia's stare widened at her mother's words. She didn't attempt to calm the woman, though. Tamara Kelly and Cora Wallace had never liked each other. They probably never would.

"Mommy, please. If you see Cora Wallace while I'm in town, can you just try and be civil?"

Tamara rolled her eyes. "It'll be a cold day in hell."

Chapter 7

"Cortez? Cortez," Renee called, when she walked into her colleague's office. The man was nowhere in sight, and Renee decided to leave. Before she reached the door she heard his voice.

"Did you tell them?"

"Cortez…"

He folded his arms across his chest and waited.

"Oh, Cortez, I couldn't. Everyone was so happy, and I know this isn't the way you wanted it, but it could be a good thing, and we—"

"Renee," he called firmly, bracing his hands upon his desk as he glared at her. "We are not engaged, and this will be an even bigger mess if we pretend to be and then it all comes out."

"Why does it have to come out?"

"Renee!" Cortez couldn't believe her.

She spread her hands defensively and drew closer to his

desk. "Just hear me out. Do you know how big we could be? We've already got quite a following for the show, but news of an engagement between coanchors on the same show? Do you have any idea of the attention we'd receive? I mean, we're talking major networks here."

As Cortez already had an offer from a major network, he wasn't nearly as excited by the prospect as Renee was. "You straighten this out or I will. Tell everyone you realized I wasn't the man for you. Then you come out on top. I don't care."

Renee fumed at his stubbornness, but she declined to argue.

A knock sounded on the door and Cortez whispered a fierce curse. "Who is it?"

"Sorry, Cortez, but Jerry in Production needs to see Renee!"

"I'll be there in a few minutes!" Renee told the production assistant. "Sorry, baby, but duty calls."

Cortez hesitated for a moment. "I won't ask again, Renee," he warned.

Renee patted the side of Cortez's scruffy cheek before she stepped around him.

"Damn it," Julia breathed, when she spotted the security station just inside the entrance of WPDM. Bracing herself for the confrontation, Julia smoothed her hands over the clinging material of her stylish black cotton dress. Stepping forward, she silently rehearsed the story she had concocted on her way to the station.

The four guards behind the tall silver counter stood a bit straighter. Their eyes gleamed with interest. The dark beauty walking toward them had their complete attention.

Julia gave the men a dazzling smile and pulled a card

from the small black purse she carried. "Hello, gentlemen. I'm Julia Kelly. I'm with Outlook TV in Los Angeles. I'm collaborating with one of your reporters, Cortez Wallace. We're supposed to meet this morning."

The men were more than happy to assist Julia.

"Yes, ma'am, that's no problem at all," one of them assured her.

"This place can be pretty confusing though." Another told her.

"Can I show you to his office?"

Julia's smile widened, as she shook her head. "Thanks, but I can find it myself if I can just get some directions?"

"Sure. It's on the twelfth floor. You take a left as soon as you leave the elevator. His office is four doors down. You'll see the receptionist."

Julia thanked the guards and made her way to the elevator.

The elevator ride was swift. When the double mahogany doors slid open, Julia found herself looking into vaguely familiar territory. Little had changed since her copyediting days there eight years ago. Of course, the station appeared no less busy than hers in L.A. It was perfect, since Julia wanted to retain as much of a low profile as possible.

She followed the directions and found the correct hall to Cortez's office.

"Excuse me?"

Lea Marquez, the receptionist for that floor, looked up from her magazine and smiled. "Hello. May I—? Julia?" she inquired.

Julia smoothed her hand across her hair. "Hey, Lea," she replied, laughing at the surprise and delight on the woman's face.

Lea rushed round to hug her. "So how can I help you

today?" she asked after she and Julia had indulged in a bit of small talk.

Julia leaned forward. "Well, I'd like to see Cortez if I could. Do you know where I could find him?"

Lea looked down the hall. "Cortez's office is through the last door on the left. You'll come to another hall and you should find Sara down there. She'll be able to help you from there."

Julia gave Lea a quick hug. "Thanks a lot," she whispered, before sauntering down the hall.

In his office, Cortez reclined in his desk chair, stroking his light beard in deep thought. The situation with Renee was almost as unsettling as the one with Julia. Almost. In truth, Renee Scales was perfect for him. Sweet, caring and willing to do whatever it took to make him happy. He doubted he'd ever come home one evening to find her bags packed and no trace of her. They could probably have a fantastic life, if only... No! Cortez commanded silently. He would not let Julia Kelly creep into his thoughts. Not now. He'd left her behind in L.A., and there she would remain.

Turning to his desk, Cortez snatched up the script for the noon broadcast. A few seconds later he was on his way to the copy department.

Julia arrived outside Cortez's office two minutes after he had left. She spotted his assistant and headed over.

"Good morning. May I help you?" Sara McBride asked, her blue eyes twinkling gaily as she smiled. "Julia?" she whispered slowly.

Julia returned the woman's smile with a dazzling one of her own. "You always were good with faces."

"Lord," Sara breathed, immediately pushing her chair

away from the pristine oak desk she sat behind. "Oooh, you look so good," she marveled while pulling Julia into a tight hug. "So what are you doing here?" She quizzed, her blue eyes sparkling with delight.

Julia shrugged, smoothing her hands across the fabric of her black dress. "My calendar was clear, so I thought I'd come see my parents. Everyone's abuzz about Cortez's engagement," she tacked on in a sly manner, deciding to keep quiet about her plans to lure WPDM's top anchor away from the fold.

Sara's eyebrows rose. "Ah, yes, the hot topic of the last several days."

Tilting her head a tad, Julia offered a tiny smirk. "Sounds like you've had to field more than your share of inquiries."

"Hmph." Sara cast a quick glance across her shoulder. "Inquiries from the general public as well as my boss."

"Oh?"

"He wasn't thrilled when that story broke," Sara said, sounding as if she'd been dying to share her confessions with someone. "He acted like it came out of nowhere."

"He couldn't have been surprised." Julia celebrated Sara's talkative nature and ordered herself not to inquire too deeply and cause the woman to clam up. But Sara was too thrilled to be discussing it all to notice she was being grilled.

"Most reporters don't like to see their own private lives turned into an open book."

Considering Julia's words, Sara leaned against her desk and then waved her hand to challenge the statement. "I don't know about that one, Julia. He was angry enough to spit nails, demanded to see Ms. Scales and everything's been pretty hush-hush since then."

Julia watched Sara absently toying with her bobbed

blond locks and steeled herself against asking any further questions.

"So are your parents here?"

Julia smiled and shook her head. "No. They're going to meet me in town for dinner later, but I stopped by to say hello to Cortez, actually." Casually, she slipped her hands into the pockets on her dress and glanced past Sara's shoulder. "Do you think it'd be okay to wait around and surprise him, if he isn't going to be away too long?"

Sara pushed away from the neat desk she leaned against and stood. "I don't see any problem with that. I don't think he'd mind, if you'd like to wait in his office."

"I'd love to," Julia said, following Sara to the double doors behind the desk.

"Can I bring you anything while you wait?" Sara asked, clasping her hands together.

"Oh, thanks, Sara, but I'm good," she replied, toying with the small gold hoop earrings she wore while taking in her surroundings.

Sara smiled and was gone from the office a moment later.

Alone in the room, Julia spent the next few minutes reading some of the plaques that covered the paneled walls of the office. It was obvious that Cortez had made a well-known, well-respected name for himself. Stepping around behind the large, imposing mahogany desk, she noticed a picture of Cortez and a woman. Renee Scales, Julia silently surmised. She could not ignore the small ache in the center of her chest as she studied the photo of the anchors accepting an award together.

Sara smiled at Cortez as she watched him head to his office. "Someone's waiting for you in there," she sang.

Cortez's hand paused over the doorknob and his chocolate stare slid over to his secretary. "Are they here to aggravate me?" he asked in a wicked tone.

"I think you'll find her too pretty to be aggravating," Sara confirmed, without looking away from her filing.

Sending Sara a strange smile, Cortez headed into his office.

Julia gasped when the door opened unexpectedly. But when her eyes landed on Cortez she quickly recovered. "Corky," she greeted perkily as she leaned against his desk.

Lord, now I'm hallucinating about the woman, Cortez silently thought. His long lashes closed over his eyes and he ran one hand across his face. Julia was still there, clear as day. She looked good. Too good. Helplessly, his deep gaze caressed every dip and curve of her body. Cortez realized what he was doing and cleared his throat.

Julia couldn't have been more pleased. She enjoyed his unease and slowly pushed herself up from behind the desk. "Aren't you going to say anything?" she softly asked, walking closer to him.

"What are you doing here?"

As though it were nothing out of the ordinary, Julia slid her arms around Cortez's neck and nuzzled her face against the base of his throat. "I'm here to do anything you want," she whispered into his ear.

Weakened by the sudden flood of arousal, Cortez let his eyes flutter closed. If possible, her perfume was even more intoxicating than it'd been in L.A. Julia could feel him responding to her and pressed her body closer to his hard, muscular frame.

Cortez finally gained control over his raging hormones and pulled away from her. "I asked you a question, Julia."

Sighing lightly, Julia smoothed her hands over her dress

and followed Cortez to his desk. "I just got into town and I thought I'd stop by and say hello," She explained, a look of surprise crossing her face when she spotted the knowing smirk on Cortez's lips. "What?"

Cortez massaged the back of his neck, as his eyes narrowed. "You came out here to change my mind, didn't you?"

Pretend outrage and shock crossed Julia's beautiful, dark face. "Change your mind?"

Cortez folded his arm across his chest and observed her closely. "Kenrick called. He said you guys weren't backing off and that you really want me out there. So they sent you to persuade me, hum?"

Julia's lips twitched into a smirk "You actually think I'd expect you to change your mind on something you feel so strongly about?" Julia smiled and sauntered closer to the desk. "Actually, my motives are purely honorable."

"Honorable?" Cortez repeated.

"I want to take you out for lunch. To celebrate." Julia explained, her narrow gaze watching him steadily.

"Celebrate?"

Julia snapped her fingers as if trying to get him to return to reality. "Your engagement."

Cortez rolled his eyes even as his wide mouth tilted upwards in a knowing smirk. "Right."

"So why didn't you tell me about it?"

"Was it your business?" he asked, focusing on his desk then.

"Well," Julia propped a hand to her hip. "Considering all the little incidents that passed between us in California…" she bit her bottom lip and let her lashes flutter at the memory. "I never would've let it go so far if I'd known."

Cortez raised his head finally, allowing his disbelief to shine through in his smoky stare.

Shaking her head, Julia sighed. "I hope you won't hold what's happened against me. What I said in California… telling you I still loved you…" she probed. "I shouldn't have said that, especially when you're about to walk down the aisle." Her gaze was subtly coy.

Cortez felt his body responding to Julia, and he looked away. In response, Julia propped herself against his desk and waited.

"Julia, lunch isn't a good idea. I need to be back on the set in a few minutes, so—"

"Maybe tomorrow then?"

"I don't think so," Cortez grimly replied, shuffling through some papers on his desk.

While his gaze was averted, Julia allowed herself to drop the vampy act. Her eyes wandered helplessly over Cortez's smooth, caramel skin, his handsome face, the long thick eyebrows, deep-set eyes, long nose, wide mouth and the light beard that shadowed his face. She could imagine herself leaning back against his powerful body, his arms encircling her waist, while his hands rose to—

"Julia?"

Her onyx stare shifted back to Cortez's face and she saw him watching her strangely. Sighing, she slid off the desk and walked around to perch herself right next to him. "I guess I'll see you tomorrow, then?" She whispered.

A suspicious frown darkened Cortez's face. "What for?" He asked.

Julia laughed at the tone of his voice. "You're right. The guys did send me out here to *persuade* you. I feel awful because you turning this opportunity down was my fault. I want to see if I can change your mind before I have to go back."

The muscle twitched so fiercely in Cortez's jaw that it could be noticed even beneath his beard. "Julia—"

"Just give me another chance to sell you on this. It's about nothing more." She cleared her throat on the lie. "Your fiancée shouldn't have a problem with that unless you haven't told her about me," Julia added, her eyes studying him closely. "And if you haven't, I wonder why?"

Cortez had no reply and simply stared at her.

Julia watched him for a moment longer before a wicked smirk crossed her face. She cupped the side of his face, her fingers caressing the crisp whiskers of his beard. When she pulled him close and pressed her lips onto his, he groaned. Julia increased the pressure of the kiss, sliding her tongue just past his lips to stroke the even ridge of his white teeth.

"Juli…" Cortez groaned beneath the onslaught of the kiss.

Julia ended the kiss by suckling his bottom lip between hers. "I'll see you tomorrow," she promised, moving away from the desk.

"Julia," Cortez called, just before she made it to the door. "Whatever you're planning, don't."

Giving him a serene smile, Julia turned and left the office.

Chapter 8

"And cut! All right, that's a wrap, folks!"

The studio instantly filled with conversation and commotion. The afternoon broadcast was finished and everyone on duty was ready to tie up last-minute details before leaving the station for the day.

"As soon as I make a few calls I'll be ready to hit the road," Renee sang as she gathered folders, pads and pens. She moved away from the news desk and noticed that Cortez wasn't following. "Hey. You okay?"

Cortez seemed to be in another world. He leaned back in his chair and sat turning it to and fro. Stroking his beard methodically, he stared into space.

"Cortez? Cortez?" Renee called, frowning until his brown gaze met hers. "What's wrong with you?"

Cortez sighed and buried his face in his hands. "I'm just worn out."

"Well that's probably because you haven't eaten today,"

Renee guessed, smiling as she patted his shoulder. She knelt beside his chair and gazed up at his gorgeous face. "Hey, why don't we go grab something? My treat."

"And how would that help to dispel all the rumors of this engagement nonsense?"

Renee's smile tightened. "You know we've shared plenty of business meals together. I'm sorry all of this is agitating our friendship, but there's little we can do to change it right now. And you've still gotta eat," she fixed him with a smug smile as he stood.

"To you, girl. As crazy and devious as you are. To you."

Julia frowned a bit as she clicked her tea glass against her sister's. "Thanks, I think."

Monique took a sip of the herbal iced-tea blend and shook her head. "You've got nerve, little sister. I have to admire that."

"I'm taking off the gloves this time," Julia said, shrugging. "Cortez is playing this engagement thing to the hilt. I'll have to play my cards just right, too."

"And you really believe it's a sham?" Monique asked, thoroughly intrigued.

Julia smoothed her hands over the soft material of her clinging dress. "It has to be."

Monique winced.

Julia noticed and leaned close to soothe her sister's concern. "Listen, I don't intend to pit myself against Renee Scales. But I will remind Cortez of what we had—of what we could have if he can get past his fears."

"Baby, are you sure that'll work?" An uneasy look crept across Monique's face.

"Mo, Cork hasn't even told the woman about me. I think that's because he's had no reason to."

"Well, you really haven't been around," Monique said after sipping her tea.

"You didn't see him in L.A." Julia chewed her thumbnail and debated.

Monique laughed. "Cortez is no fool. And you won't be able to use business as your ticket in for long."

"I agree," Julia said, not offended by the statement. "But Cortez doesn't trust himself around me. He doesn't trust me. I have to find a way to change that."

"Come again?"

Julia smoothed her hand over her sleek, short hair. "In California he told me that he couldn't survive taking me back just to lose me again. So I know this engagement is a sham, Mo. I've got to prove to him that I don't want to go anywhere unless it's with him. So I'll see how far he plans to drag out this engagement lie while I remain my usual sexy self. He won't be able to resist me, and then he won't even know what hit him."

Monique threw her head back and laughed. "Girl, you are too much."

Julia's only reply was a shrug and smug smile.

Just then, Cortez and Renee were arriving at the same restaurant where Julia and her sister were dining.

"You'll feel a lot better after you eat something," Renee assured Cortez as they walked through the heavy mahogany doors of Luchini's Italian Eatery.

"Right," Cortez grunted, as he followed Renee to the hostess booth. As Renee talked to the young woman about a table, Cortez looked around the spacious yet crowded restaurant. The atmosphere was very cool and laid-back. Rays of sunlight beamed in through the huge windows, showering the casually set tables with warm light. Cortez was feeling better just standing there and taking in the view. That all changed, though, the instant he saw Julia Kelly. His heart slammed against his chest as he watched her. He'd never met a woman so confident, or one who could pull his strings so fiercely.

"Well, Ms. Scales, the only table I have at the moment is in the rear section of the restaurant. Will that do?"

Renee sighed and thought about it for a second. "Cortez, what do you think?"

Cortez's unwavering stare was still focused across the room.

"Cortez?"

"Hmm?" He absently replied. "I'm sorry, what?"

Renee frowned and watched him closely for a moment. "I was asking if you thought we should wait for a table or take the one they have in the back."

"Where is that?" Cortez instantly asked. He wouldn't be able to eat a thing sitting across from Julia.

The hostess smiled at the handsome man before her. "It's right over there," she said, pointing to the lone empty table, far from where Julia was seated.

"We'll take it." Cortez decided.

"You sure?" Renee asked.

"Positive," Cortez assured Renee, pulling her along with him.

"Lord, he is still so incredible to look at," Monique mentioned to her sister.

"You're so right," Julia agreed. She had spotted Cortez as soon as he had stepped to the hostess booth.

"Who was that woman with him?"

"His fiancée," Julia confirmed lightly, taking a bite of a breadstick.

Monique frowned. "She looks totally different than on TV, but I thought you said you'd never met the woman?"

One of Julia's eyebrows arched a bit more. "I haven't," she said, remembering the photo she had seen in Cortez's office. "But I'm about to." She pushed her chair away from the table.

"You know you're starting to worry me here? Can you at least try to tell me what's wrong? I've got a feeling it's about more than our sham engagement," Renee pleaded. They had just placed their orders and were attempting to enjoy their drinks.

Cortez flashed her his trademark sexy grin and shook his head. "I appreciate you being concerned, but I'm fine."

Renee toyed with a lock of her hair. "You don't see what I do. You're acting so…distant."

"I told you I wasn't in the mood to eat," he muttered while staring at the menu.

"Cortez, what's the harm in playing this out?" Renee hissed and then glanced around to see if anyone was watching them. "It's not like we're in other relationships or anything."

Cortez massaged the back of his neck. "This isn't the conversation we need to have right now," he warned. "Just don't worry about me, all right?"

"The two of you make a beautiful couple."

Cortez instantly recognized the voice from above. His head snapped up and he looked right into Julia's twinkling, dark gaze.

"Not here, Julia," he snapped.

Julia overlooked his chilly words and smiled at Renee. "Hi. How are you? My name is Julia Kelly. Cortez and I are old friends, and I just wanted to congratulate you on your engagement," she said, offering Renee her hand.

"Thank you so much." Renee said, smiling brightly as she shook Julia's hand. "Why don't you join us?"

"Renee—"

"Thanks, Renee, but I don't want to barge in on you. I would like to invite you both to dinner one night this week, though."

"We're real busy, Julia," Cortez interrupted.

"Honey, we're not too busy to have dinner with one of your old friends," Renee insisted.

Cortez's heavy brows drew close into a frown as he sat massaging his temple. "We can do it another time, Julia. After the wedding," he added sarcastically.

Renee tried to maintain her smile. "Honey, you act like you don't want me and Julia to be friends."

Julia remained silent and stood watching Cortez with a knowing little smile on her lovely, dark face.

"Julia probably has a lot to do before the end of her trip."

"Well, that's all the more reason for us to get together, Cork, uh, Cortez," Julia pointed out, intentionally fumbling over his name.

Instead of responding, Cortez decided to give up the fight. When he began shaking his head, Julia nodded and dipped into her purse.

"This is my card," she said, writing her hotel name and phone number on the back.

As soon as Julia placed the card on the table, Cortez picked it up. He scanned the address on the back before handing it to Renee.

"I'll be sure to call," Renee promised.

"Well, I'll look forward to it." Julia gave Cortez a brief but intense stare. "You two enjoy your meal," she said, smiling at Renee once more before she walked away.

Cortez could not stop his eyes from following Julia. Her slow, seductive stride held him entranced.

"Cortez, what is it with you?" Renee scolded. "I've never seen you act so nasty with anyone. Especially a woman."

Cortez was silent for a long while. "That woman has been my nemesis, you could say, for years. She's always rubbed me the wrong way."

Renee laughed, thoroughly tickled by the confession. "Well, honey, ya'll are grown now. Julia seems to be making a serious effort."

If you only knew, Cortez thought. "Can we just change the conversation?"

Later that evening Julia was back in her hotel room. She was smoothing on some lotion after her bath when the phone began to ring.

"Hello?" Julia answered after the third ring.

"Hi, it's Renee Scales."

"Oh, Renee, hi," Julia greeted politely, surprised to hear the woman's voice.

"I was calling to see if you'd like to have dinner with us tonight. We're eating with Cortez's mother," Renee explained.

Dinner with Cora Wallace was the absolute last thing Julia felt like doing. "I don't want to intrude."

"Oh, Cora won't mind."

"Thanks, Renee, but Cora Wallace and I don't get along that well."

"Oh, well, I'm sorry to hear that," Renee softly stated the disappointment evident in her voice. "Well listen, why don't we go *out* for dinner? I'm sure you don't want to stay cooped up in that hotel room the whole time you're here."

"You're right, I don't," Julia assured Renee, laughing. "Going out somewhere sounds great, just tell me when and where."

"Well, tomorrow's good for us, if you don't have anything planned."

"Tomorrow's fine."

"Good. How about seven? Gravely's Seafood?"

"That sounds good. I'll see you then."

"Okay. Well, we'll talk to you then. Bye."

Julia stared at the phone for a moment after hanging up. She thought about how nice Renee seemed. She hoped they wouldn't become friends, but she feared that might happen. If it did, how would she view this supposed sham engagement?

The doorbell rang, interrupting Julia's thoughts. She shook her head, cursing herself for being affected by something so trivial. Rushing to her closet, she pulled out a cream silk robe and hurried to the door.

The surprise guest had abandoned the doorbell and started to pound on the door. Julia stopped in the middle of the living room, frowning toward the entryway.

"Would you stop with the pounding? I'm coming!" she bellowed, tying the robe's belt around her waist. Stomping to the door, she whipped it open.

Cortez stormed into the room, a fierce glare on his gorgeous face.

"Corky." Julia greeted in a breathless tone.

Cortez was in a frightful mood and had to take several deep breaths before he spoke. "I want to know what the hell you're doing here. I want the truth from you this time."

A tiny smirk tugged at Julia's full lips and she glanced around. "This is my hotel room, remember?"

Cortez wasn't in the mood for games and quickly closed

the space between them. His iron grip closed around her upper arms and he jerked her toward him. "Don't," he softly ordered.

Julia swallowed and looked him steadily in the eyes. "I haven't done anything to get you this upset. I'm tryin' to be civil with you, damn it. I even came with a job offer."

Cortez winced, his anger refusing to remain at bay. "What about in my office?"

Julia laughed. "Surely Renee wouldn't mind two friends embracing from time to time?"

"I mind," Cortez whispered, pulling Julia even closer.

The fierce expression on Cortez's face didn't frighten her. Giving him a purely devilish smile, she curled her fingers around the lapels of his stylish cotton jacket. "Then let me give you something to really care about."

Julia pressed her lips against Cortez's. She slipped her tongue inside his mouth and kissed him with infinite gentleness and passion combined. The kiss became hotter, wetter. Cortez was so unprepared by the rush of sensation that he groaned.

Julia cupped the back of his head in her palm and added more pressure to the kiss. She felt the insistent bulge beneath Cortez's trousers and shivered.

"Take this off," she whispered, trying to pull the jacket off his back.

Cortez stiffened against Julia and pushed her away. He held her at arm's length, staring at her for a long while. His brown eyes smoldered with need and arousal, before his lips crashed down on hers again.

Julia wasn't frightened by the sheer force behind the action. She welcomed it. It was as though Cortez were starved for her. The kiss was deep, hot and lusty. As his hands caressed her back through the silk robe she wore, Julia feared her legs would give out beneath her. She knew nothing other than pure male arousal controlled his actions, but she couldn't deny her…happiness.

Finally, though, something seemed to snap, and Cortez tore away from her. He took only a few moments to catch his breath before he stormed out of the room. The door slammed shut behind him.

Julia stood rooted in place and watched the door with wide eyes. When she touched her bruised lips she dropped to the sofa.

Chapter 9

"Aw, man! Come on! What the hell are ya'll doin'?"

The sounds of male laughter and conversation filled Correll Wallace's house. The men had gotten together for the basketball playoffs and were eagerly anticipating their team's triumph. The guys had chosen their spots before the flat-screen TV. Chips, dip, beer and other snacks covered the long oak coffee table in the center of the room.

When Cortez knocked on his brother's door around 9:30, no one answered. Grimacing, Cortez pounded harder on the door. Then, remembering his brother had given him a key, he let himself inside.

Cortez walked into the house without being noticed right away. But as soon as a commercial came on and the guys spotted him they were greeting him heartily.

"Hey, it's the celebrity!" Kyle Jackson was saying.

Cortez laughed and waved at his brother's friends. He knew their teasing was all in fun, but tonight he couldn't enjoy it. Cortez caught his brother's eye and nodded. "Can we talk?" He mouthed, tilting his head toward the kitchen.

Correll took another swig from the beer bottle in his hand before pushing himself out of his armchair. He followed his younger brother into the kitchen, watching him closely. "What's up?" he asked, a look of expectancy on his handsome face.

"She's back," Cortez blurted.

"She's back…? Can you clarify that, my man?"

Cortez sighed. "Julia. Julia Kelly's back in Detroit."

"Well, I'll be damned," Correll murmured, lightly stroking his jaw.

Cortez rolled his eyes toward the ceiling. "She looks even better than she used to, and it's hard turning her away. You know what I mean?" Cortez asked, turning his concerned stare toward his brother.

Correll nodded at the suggestive statement. His light complexion reddened slightly.

"I didn't tell you about my California trip," Cortez began to explain. "Talk about not being able to turn her away. She was everywhere. Then she shows up here in town under the guise of wanting to talk about the position they want to offer me in Cali—"

"And you figure there's more to it than that, right?" Correll asked, his sleek brows raised high above his dark brown eyes.

"There is." He remembered what had just happened and took a swig of Correll's beer. "Trust me, there is."

Correll walked to the tall chrome refrigerator at the back of the kitchen. "So why are you so upset?" he asked, grabbing a bowl of grapes from the top shelf.

"Man. It's Julia."

Correll shrugged, his attention focused on the bowl of fruit. "And? You're getting married, right?"

Cortez groaned and decided he had to at least tell his brother the truth. "The engagement is a scam. Someone speculated there might be more going on between us and Renee ran with it." Cortez propped one hand against his hip and glared at his brother.

"And you haven't corrected the lie?"

Cortez closed his eyes and massaged the bridge of his nose. "Right now I think it's better for Julia to think I'm off limits."

"I don't get it," Correll admitted, raising his narrowed eyes from the bowl of grapes.

"If she accepts the engagement, maybe she'll leave town and...I just can't go through the drama with her again, man."

"She's still makin' it clear that she wants you?" Correll guessed.

"Exactly."

"Hmph." Correll gestured, popping a plump grape into his mouth. "Well, like you said, it's Julia. What's the harm in a little teasing?"

Cortez braced his large hands against the paneled countertop. "You know what the harm is. I can't handle Julia's type of teasing. Never have been able to."

"Well it's time you learn how. She's just messin' with you."

"I kissed her."

Correll shrugged. "So she kissed you. No big deal."

"No. *I* kissed *her.*"

"Cortez."

"I know. I didn't mean to. She was just acting so cool about everything, while I'm standing over there mad as hell. She kissed me first and I pushed her away, but—"

"You couldn't resist for long?" Correll finished watching his brother shake his head. "You know, Renee is a great lady, Tez."

"Yeah…you, Ma and everyone else remind me of that as often as you all can." Cortez whispered.

"It's worth keeping in mind," Correll advised.

"Hey, you buckin' for a promotion?" Renee teased Cortez when she found him in his office bright and early the next morning.

Cortez dropped the folder in his hands and stood. "Work keeps me out of trouble."

"We're due back on the set," Renee reminded him.

Cortez checked his watch, grimacing at the time before rounding his desk to meet Renee.

"We've got a dinner date with Julia tonight," Renee lightly announced, when she and Cortez had taken their seats behind the news desk.

Cortez's striking brown eyes snapped to Renee. "What? Why didn't you tell me?"

"I just did."

"Renee…"

"In five, four, three, two…"

Thrown, Cortez stumbled just slightly over his opening statements. He knew that it was going to be a very long day.

"Can you repeat that, please?"

Julia watched her mother set her coffee mug on the table and sighed. "I said I'm having dinner with Renee and Cortez tonight."

"And whose idea was that?" Tamara knowingly asked.

"Renee's," Julia instantly replied, nodding curtly at her mother's shocked expression.

"And you're going?" Tamara asked, very suspicious of the invitation.

Julia shrugged. "Why wouldn't I?"

"His fiancée will be there, too," Tamara reminded her daughter.

"I'll deal with that," Julia flippantly replied, grimacing when Tamara shook her head and sighed. "Mommy, please," she began, knowing the woman was concerned. "I'm not out to hurt anybody, but I have to know if there's something, anything, before I forget him for good this time."

"Baby, hasn't he given you the answer to that question many times?" Tamara asked, looking directly into Julia's dark eyes. "I just wish I could figure out Renee's reasoning in all this," she added.

"Her reasoning?"

Tamara waved off Julia's question. "Little girl, I don't know any woman who would want to go out with her fiancé and his young, beautiful, ex-whatever."

Julia smoothed her hand across the back of her sleek hair. "I think that's it right there. She's as curious about me as I am about her."

"You're his past. She's his present and future. That's all either of you need to know."

Julia shook her head. "It's not that simple, Ma."

"Well, this whole thing seems real funny to me, so you just be careful."

Julia leaned across the counter and squeezed her mother's hand. "I have every intention of doing that."

Cortez rushed into his office and threw the folder he carried to his desk. He picked up the phone and quickly punched in seven digits.

"Correll Wallace's office." A pleasant voice answered.

"Hey, Lila, is my brother around?"

Lila Harris's smile widened when she heard Cortez's voice. "He sure is. I'll put you right through."

"Correll Wallace."

"How about dinner tonight, man?" Cortez sighed and dropped to the leather chair behind his desk. "I need you to go with me and Renee tonight."

"You need me to? Why?"

"Renee invited Julia to have dinner out with us tonight."

Correll whistled and pulled the thin-framed spectacles from his face. "And you need me to take some of the spotlight off you?"

"You mind?"

"Well, I still think you're overreacting about the girl."

"Okay, well now you can see for yourself that I'm not."

"Hell, does Julia Kelly know how easy it is for her to unsettle you?"

Cortez couldn't help but grin. "Damn right she does. That's the problem."

Correll laughed. "What the hell. It might be fun."

Julia was determined to wear something that would dazzle but not be overly suggestive. She decided to buy a new outfit and took a trip to one of Detroit's many shopping centers.

It didn't take long to find something eye-catching. The pearl-gray dress reached just above her knee. The sleeves were long and flaring with a scooped neckline that revealed glimpses of ample bosom.

"What do you think?"

The store's assistant manager smiled at Julia. "Honey, whoever he is, his eyes are gonna be working overtime tonight."

Julia laughed and turned back toward the full-length mirror. She couldn't mask the wicked giggle that glided up her throat.

"My, my, Julia Kelly."

The instant Julia heard Cora Wallace's voice she uttered a silent curse. Closing her eyes, she took a deep breath.

"Honey, I know that's you. Aren't you going to speak?"

"Hello, Cora," Julia replied, whirling around to face the woman.

Cora Wallace's smile was undeniably phony. Her eyes, however, sparkled with interest and curiosity. "My, my. Imagine seeing you here…now."

"Yeah, my mother's very happy to have me home," Julia coolly replied, ignoring Cora's sarcasm.

"I'll bet she was surprised."

Julia nodded. "She was."

Cora's cool stare took in Julia's attire briefly before snapping away. "You're looking good. I never would've known you were here if I hadn't heard your voice."

"I'm flattered you recognized it," Julia said through clenched teeth.

"You shouldn't be," Cora corrected her. "It's hard to forget a voice that's always tying up your phone lines."

"I haven't called your home once in over eight years," Julia informed the older woman. She didn't bother to hide the distaste in her voice this time.

Cora shrugged. "Well, I'm sure you managed to track him down elsewhere."

"All right, Cora, you listen to me—"

"No, you listen. I'm warning you. Don't interfere with my son's life. He's happy and engaged to a lovely lady."

Julia winced at the obvious insult, but she didn't turn away as Cora continued.

"I am so glad he's so happy and in love with Renee. This wedding is going to go off with no problems and I want you to stay away from him," Cora viciously ordered.

Julia took a step toward Cora, her onyx stare blazing. "It'll be pretty hard to stay away when I'm having dinner with him tonight."

Cora smarted as though she had been slapped. "How'd you manage that?" she whispered in an accusing tone.

Julia turned and headed toward the dressing rooms. "You should ask your soon-to-be daughter-in-law."

Cora's eyes narrowed as she stood shaking her head at Julia's departure.

Chapter 10

"**K**en, I'm just advising you to prepare yourself and the guys for the worst. Cortez Wallace can be a stubborn man." *I should know,* Julia thought silently while speaking with Kenrick Owen that afternoon. "I may not be able to woo him into accepting our offer."

"It isn't like you to be so pessimistic, Julia," Ken threw back, not bothering to hide his amusement. "I think the fact that you've met your match is why we're so eager to get Cortez out here. Heaven knows no else has the nerve to stand up to you."

"I'm hanging up Ken." Julia's thumb was poised over the cellular's end button.

"Listen, you haven't met with him yet, right?"

Julia hesitated on the answer when she saw Cortez walking into the quiet dining room of the restaurant where they'd agreed to meet for lunch.

"I just want you guys to understand he's no pushover."

Her words caught in her throat when he looked in her direction as the host pointed. "A pretty face with no substance—that's not him," she finished. "I'll be in touch." She ended the connection just as Cortez headed for the table.

"Thanks for showing up," Julia said when he approached. "I know it's the last place you want to be." She folded her arms across her navy suit coat in an effort to appear at ease.

Cortez took his seat, not bothering with a reply. She'd be stunned to hear him tell her he'd rather be there than at the station being congratulated at every turn over his phony engagement. "Well, you've got me curious."

Julia waved a hand when the waiter inquired about refreshing her drink. "Curious? Could you be more specific? There's so much to choose from," she teased once he'd ordered a Sam Adams.

Cortez crossed his long legs at the ankles when he reclined in the chair he occupied across from Julia. "Do you really have more to discuss about the Haven offer, or is this a joke?"

Leaning forward, Julia smirked. "You mean will I try anything to be alone with you?" she clarified and watched him shrug. "My, you have gotten conceited over the last eight years. Letting your most eligible bachelor status go to your head, huh?"

"Been pleased to wear it for eight years." He smiled.

"Better not let your fiancée hear that." The cool in her expression became something far more intense when she spied the sharpening of his gorgeous features. "Nothing I say or do with you is a joke, pretense or show to prove a point, Cortez."

"What about dinner tonight with Renee?"

"Call it curiosity."

Cortez thanked the waiter as he arrived with his beer and allowed Julia's response to settle without rebuke. "The guys laid out a pretty impressive offer. I don't see how they could top it," he said, while tugging on the cuff of his moss jacket sleeve.

Julia relaxed in her chair, happy to return the conversation to business. "They've still got a few tricks up their sleeves. I'm here to reiterate that proposal and remind you of what a coup it could be for your career."

"A coup, huh?" He took a swig of the dark brew and grinned. "I wonder about that, seeing as how you were so sure it'd fail."

"I'll admit that was my own anger talking." Julia nodded, tapping her nails against the stout beaded glass before her. "It's a good concept, Cortez. Showing people the grittiness of a city known for glamour and stardom. Uncovering the fake beauty to get to the ugly places and ugly events that are too much of its reality is what this show has the power to do. It's gonna fly, no matter who's in front of the camera. I just think having a woman in those gritty situations would be far more interesting for the audience."

Cortez laughed. "Putting a woman smack dab in the middle of a war zone would get more ratings, is that it?"

"Surely," Julia agreed, raising her glass in toast before drinking from it. She took no offense when Cortez laughed and called her ruthless. "I can see you're as much of a chauvinist as my male colleagues," she accused.

Shrugging, Cortez tapped his bottle to the table. "I don't mind wearing the label. It just doesn't sit well with me, putting a woman in that situation."

It was Julia's turn to laugh. "She's not out there on her own, you know?"

"Things happen," he challenged, taking a deep swig of his beer.

"Yes, they do." Julia considered. Her dark gaze fell to her nearly empty glass and she regretted not ordering a refill earlier. Suddenly, the discussion was weaving its way back toward topics best left alone. "Anyway," she forced an airy tone to her voice, "I'll be very happy for the opportunity to prove you all wrong."

"Once my show fails?"

Julia hid her smile at the unconscious possessiveness in his statement. "Actually, your acceptance is something I want very much, since they're now willing to pit the shows against each other on two of their largest networks."

"Congratulations." Cortez's voice had a touch of surprise mingled in its deep octave. "Is it always so easy to bend them into doing what you want?"

She couldn't pull her eyes from the powerful hands on the bottle he held. "Well, they can't deny my record." She leaned forward to shrug out of the suit coat that was suddenly stifling her. "It speaks for itself, and this particular idea just hit 'em below the belts."

A muscle danced along Cortez's jaw. He took the last swallow of his drink and studied the line of her collarbone and the heave of her breasts more easily visible once she'd removed the jacket. "Guess you made the right choice when you headed out to L.A."

"It wasn't a choice," she shared, intrigued by the way his eyes lingered on the rise and fall of her chest. "It wasn't a choice," she repeated when he was looking at her face. "It was a decision made on the spur of a very ugly moment."

Cortez's long, sleek brows drew close as his anger began to be stoked. "Why didn't you tell me what you heard? Why didn't you trust me enough to face it with you?"

"Face it *with* me? And *against* who? Remember, Cortez, this is *your* family we're talking about."

His fist clenched. "*You* were my family."

"Sorry for keeping you waiting, Mr. Wallace." The waiter arrived slightly out of breath. Julia welcomed the interruption since it was no exaggeration to say she was speechless.

"The guys added a few more incentives to sweeten the pot," she said, once their lunch orders were taken. "Could we focus on that?"

Cortez only waved a hand, silently urging her to continue.

"I'm coming!" Renee shouted in the direction of the phone. She had been hurrying to get ready for dinner when the steady ringing began.

"Renee? Is that you?" Cora Wallace asked when she heard the girl's breathless voice.

"Oh, hi, Cora. I'm just trying to get ready for dinner over here."

"Honey, please tell me you and Cortez are eating alone."

Renee frowned at the almost frantic tone in Cora's voice. "Well, no. We're going out with one of Cortez's old friends."

"Julia Kelly?"

"Yeah, but how did you—"

"Honey, what were you thinking inviting that girl out with you and Cortez?"

"Relax, Cora. I only wanted to get to know Julia better."

"You're makin' a mistake with this one, Renee," Cora cautioned.

Renee smiled and shook her head. "I think you're overreacting."

"You don't know Julia Kelly. She's been infatuated with Cortez her entire life."

"That may be, but Cortez is marrying *me*." Renee commended herself on the ease with which she spoke the lie.

Cora gave a short, humorless laugh. "Speaking of the wedding, you might want to consider moving it up a few weeks."

"Good night, Cora," Renee laughed, before hanging up.

Cortez attacked the tablecloth at Gravely's Seafood with soft stabs of his knife.

Renee sighed and covered his hand with hers. "What is your problem?"

Cortez shook his head as his eyes narrowed. "This dinner isn't one of your best ideas."

"Cortez, is there anything you'd like to talk about?" Renee asked, after watching him very closely.

"Anything like what?"

"Anything about you and Julia Kelly," Renee asked, absently tugging at the collar of her lightweight red coat dress. "Obviously there's a lot of history there. And you've really been on edge. I'm assuming she's got a lot to do with it."

Cortez massaged the bridge of his nose. It'd be nice to put it all on Julia, but combined with this lie he was letting Renee get away with, there was much more feeding his agitation. He'd called himself a fool many times over for not ending the whole damn mess. Now he had to deal with these lingering feelings that Julia was re-stirring. He could only hope by dragging out the charade that Julia would accept that he was off limits and give up. She had to. Telling her he wouldn't survive if she left him again wasn't just his play at drama. It was the truth.

Renee smiled and didn't press Cortez to be more forthcoming. For show, and a fair amount of her own desire, she smoothed a kiss against his hair-roughened cheek. "Why don't you put that aside tonight and enjoy the evening?" she whispered, looking up past Cortez. "We're all here."

Cortez raised his sensual chocolate stare and saw Julia heading toward the booth. He grasped his lower lip between his teeth to keep his mouth from gaping open. The dress she wore emphasized every curve and natural attribute she had. It was obvious to Cortez that the dress was worn to make him uncomfortable. Stubbornly, he refused to give her the satisfaction of knowing she had achieved her goal.

"Hey, guys. Sorry I'm late," Julia breathlessly apologized, taking her seat at the table. She wanted to keep her eyes off Cortez, but it was hopeless. Her sparkling dark gaze was intense and steady.

"Oh don't worry about it. We should go ahead and order," Renee suggested.

Cortez realized that his gaze was trained on Julia's chest and he looked away. "We should wait a while, since someone else is coming."

Renee frowned. "Who?"

"I invited Correll."

"Oh," Renee whispered, surprised by the information. She looked over at Julia, who seemed just as surprised, and smiled. "I better go snag a waiter to set another place."

"Where are you going?" Cortez asked, grabbing Renee's hand when she stood.

"The waiter—"

"He'll be over in a minute."

Renee patted Cortez on the cheek. "I better get him before it gets any more crowded."

Julia waited until Renee had left, to slide closer to Cortez in the cozy booth. "Are you afraid of something?"

"What?" Cortez asked, his brown eyes snapping to her face.

Julia shrugged one shoulder lazily. "I don't know. Maybe about being here with me and Renee."

Cortez leaned his head against the cushioned back of the booth. "I thought it'd be nicer to have four instead of three."

"No, you just thought it would be easier."

Slowly, Cortez opened his eyes and watched her unblinkingly. Julia returned the gesture and waited for his response. Finally a slow, devious smirk tugged at her full lips.

A grimace clouded Cortez's gorgeous face and he glared at her. "You're gonna push me too far in a minute," he whispered, giving her a firm, warning glare.

Julia gasped playfully, "I hope so."

"Sorry I'm late."

Julia and Cortez looked up when Correll's voice floated down over them. Cortez smiled the moment he saw his brother.

Julia's gaze faltered briefly, but she managed a shaky smile.

"Girl, Tez told me you were back in town," Correll whispered in Julia's ear as he hugged her. "His descriptions didn't even come close."

Julia graced Correll with a dazzling smile and

dismissed the memories of the words of warning she'd heard him give his brother all those years ago. Her gaze snapped to Cortez's face. "His descriptions? Well, how far off base were they?"

Correll had taken his seat. "I guess they weren't really that far. He said you were still fine as hell, but I'm just glad I saw for myself."

Cortez had been silent, studying Julia intently. The sparkle in her onyx eyes when she laughed, the healthy, even tone of her dark skin and the blatant sexuality that surrounded her were impossible to ignore.

"Correll! This is such a surprise!"

Renee had finally arrived back at the table with the waiter. She took her seat and leaned over to kiss Correll's cheek.

"What's goin' on, girl?" Correll asked, leaning back to allow the waiter to set his place.

Renee shrugged and fiddled with a tendril of hair that dangled outside her high ponytail. "Not much, just trying to keep my head above water while I'm planning this wedding."

Correll's laughter was full and honest in light of the fact that he already knew the entire business was a lie. "Is it getting to you?"

Renee smiled and glanced at Cortez. "Sometimes, but it's worth it for this guy," she said, favoring Cortez with an adoring smile.

Julia suddenly felt a tightening across her chest and began to cough. Reaching for her glass, she took several deep gulps. Many times during dinner, she raised her eyes to find Cortez watching her. She wondered if he was aware of the intensity of his gorgeous brown stare. Whether he was or not, it didn't matter to Julia. She found herself having a rather nice time. Despite the circumstances, the evening passed quite enjoyably. In no time, the foursome was ordering dessert.

"So, Correll, I hear you're part of the ad game." Julia's dark eyes were alive with interest as she watched the man nod.

"Started it shortly after Dad passed."

Julia watched Correll drink his gin while she recalled the death of Andre Wallace, whose heart problems had finally gotten the better of him. He passed shortly after opening his seventh Detroit area dealership.

"I was more interested in being an entrepreneur like our dad." Correll slanted a soft look toward his brother. "It was more about that than the actual advertising." His broad shoulders rose beneath his cream shirt when he shrugged. "But I've got a few skills there, so—"

"I'd say you've got more than a few," Julia commended. "I've seen billboards, heard radio and TV spots about Correll Marketing practically every day since I got to town."

"He's everywhere," Renee raved.

"Not everywhere." Correll grinned bashfully. "Not everywhere. But I intend to be," he added in a more meaningful tone. "That's where I'm hoping you'll come in, Julia."

She choked on her drink and fixed him with a frown. "Me?"

"Exposure on a national level," he clarified, leaning over to pat her back. "Outlook TV would be a prime place to begin."

Julia nodded her agreement. "It'll cost you," she warned, "but if you're willing to spend the money, I'm confident we could make you plenty more."

Laughter resounded at the table, and everyone raised their glasses to toast.

"Well, now that that's settled, I'm going to excuse myself to the ladies' room, you guys," Renee announced, before the coffee and cheesecake arrived.

Julia stood, as well. "I'll go with you."

The brothers watched Julia and Renee walk away. Correll waited until they were out of sight before he spoke.

"Interesting."

Cortez chased an ice cube in his glass. "What?" he asked, without raising his eyes.

"This dinner. I've never seen you look so uncomfortable, man."

"Not uncomfortable, just ready to get the hell out of here," Cortez responded, his baritone voice sounding raspy.

Correll raised his eyes toward the ceiling. "What the hell for? You got two fine women here for you. Julia is lookin' good."

"And that's about the fifth time you told me that," Cortez noted drily, not hearing the edge in his own voice.

Correll propped his fist beneath his chin and studied his sibling for a long while. "'Listen, little brother. Are you as upset with Julia as you pretend to be?"

"As I pretend to be?"

"Come on, you know what I mean."

Cortez leaned back in his chair and rolled his eyes. "Whatever," he sighed, with a flippant wave of his hand.

Correll made no further comment and just watched his younger brother brood. He noticed that Cortez never answered his question.

"Do you know Correll well, too, Julia?" Renee asked, as she rinsed her hands in the porcelain sink.

Julia sighed, checking her hair in the mirror. "Pretty well."

"He's as handsome as his brother," Renee noted, her brown eyes twinkling.

Julia could imagine where the conversation might lead. She had no desire to let Renee try matchmaking her to Correll. "He's all right."

Fortunately, Renee didn't press the issue. She reapplied her lipstick and checked her high ponytail. Smiling, she turned back to Julia. "Well, I'm headed back out. Are you ready?"

"You go ahead, I'll be right out." Julia said, pretending to be searching in her purse for something.

When the swinging door to the ladies' room closed, Julia ceased her phony search. She leaned against the marble counter and thought about Renee Scales. The woman seemed so nice. Perhaps she *was* good for Cortez. Quickly, Julia shook off her uncertainties. She checked her makeup and then headed out of the restroom.

Cortez was on his way to the restroom just as Julia entered the hallway. They didn't make eye contact and had almost passed each other. Julia pressed her lips together and tried like hell, but she couldn't keep quiet.

"Let me know if you need a hand," she offered softly.

Losing the feather hold on his temper, Cortez grabbed Julia's arm. None too gently, he hauled her against the wall. "I want you to get the hell out of here," he whispered coldly.

Julia ignored the sinking feeling in her stomach at his words. She did not look away, though. Instead, she trailed one finger over the crisp, black whiskers of his beard. Her dark eyes traced his fantastic features and a small smile tugged at her lips. "You really are scared of me, aren't you?"

Cortez didn't answer, but his cold stare faltered. Julia leaned close to study him more intently. What she saw there in his eyes seemed to weaken her resolve, and she blinked in realization. Without another word, she turned and walked away.

When Cortez arrived back at the table, he found Correll, Renee and Julia laughing. Everyone appeared to be having a great time, but Cortez had lost what little desire he had to socialize. One large hand curled around Renee's arm, and he pulled her up from the table.

"We're leaving," he announced.

"Good night," Julia called, not wanting to make a scene by commenting on the abrupt departure. She received a smile from Renee and a glare from Cortez.

"See ya, Renee," Correll said.

Cortez nodded. "Talk to you later."

"They sure make a nice couple," Correll noted, watching his brother and Renee leave the restaurant.

Julia was still watching Cortez and did not realize anything had been said. Her dark gaze, though intense, held no trace of sadness.

"Julia?" Correll said softly, waving one hand before her eyes.

Correll laughed at the confused look on Julia's lovely, dark face. "I was saying Cortez and Renee make a nice couple."

Julia looked away and closed her eyes. "Yeah, they sure do."

"Hey, are you okay?" Correll asked, leaning closer.

"Yeah. I'm fine," Julia assured him, though she

was close to tears. "I should get out of here, too," she whispered, rising from the table.

"Wait a minute," Correll called, following her through the restaurant. "Can I offer you a ride back to your hotel or something?"

"No, I have a car," Julia replied hurriedly.

"Well, how about having a drink with me before you call it a night? We can discuss my venture with your network."

Julia stopped and turned. She gave Correll a soft smile, but shook her head. "Maybe some other time?"

Correll pressed a kiss to her cheek and returned the smile. "Sure."

On her way out of the restaurant, Julia took time to ponder Correll Wallace's hospitality. Oh, he'd never been blatantly ugly to her the way his mother was. She figured that had more to do with the fact that he imagined himself finding his way into her bed once his brother was done with her. While any involvement was out of the question between her and Correll, Julia couldn't help but admit she was doing herself a disservice turning away the many men who dotted her doorstep. If only she weren't so consumed by Cortez Wallace... For the first time in a long time Julia admitted to herself that her love and wants might not be enough to sway what was clearly a dead issue.

Chapter 11

"I thought you'd be walking on cloud nine after last night."

Julia sent her sister a weary look and buried her face in her hands. "I should've stayed home."

"That bad, huh?" Monique asked, taking a seat next to Julia on the sofa.

Julia groaned in response, leaning back against the cushiony sofa.

"Well, what happened? Can I have some details?" Monique propped her hand beneath her chin and glared at her younger sister.

"I've done everything I can think of to get Corky to change his mind about us. But he won't. He's set on making me see that it's over."

Monique appeared to be confused. "A few short hours ago, that would've spurred you on. I don't get why you're so down."

"I'm having doubts," Julia admitted, moving off the sofa.

"Come again?"

Julia massaged her neck. "Maybe I shouldn't be doing this. I should probably go on back to L.A. I can imagine the work that's cluttering my desk back there."

"I see." Monique sighed. "So you thought of this when? Between the time you saw him in the hallway and back at the dinner table?"

Julia smiled in spite of herself. "I just started thinking about what I said to Cortez. I told him I thought he was afraid of me, of what I made him feel."

"And?"

Julia took a deep breath and turned away from Monique. "And then I thought if he is afraid, maybe it's because he really does love Renee and he doesn't want any old emotions to jeopardize what he's got with her."

Monique stood from the sofa and walked over to Julia. Gently, she turned her sister away from the window. "If that's true, what does it mean for you?"

Julia blinked, sending a lone tear down her cheek. "The only thing I ever wanted is for Cortez to be happy. All this time I hoped he'd find that with me. Now he's found someone he actually wants to marry. It's high time for me to admit that maybe this wasn't meant to be." Julia sniffed and wiped her tears away with the back of her hand. "Besides," she continued, "Renee's a great woman. She really is. She's sweet, kind and she loves him a lot. I can't hurt her like this. If she makes Cortez happy, then I'll just have to accept that, right?"

Monique's brown eyes were wide as she watched the lovely young woman before her. "I can't believe I'm hearing you say this."

Julia shrugged her shoulders and gave a shaky laugh. "Trust me, Mo, I find it hard to believe myself."

On the other side of town, Cortez lay in bed thinking about last night. His eyes stared out into space, as his palm glided over the smooth, wide surface of his chest. In the solitude of his own home, he could admit it. The truth was that he had been fooling himself for a long time about his feelings for Julia. He had always loved her. That fire, spirit, the sex appeal that exuded itself in her every move. The aggressive, take-charge attitude that was something he didn't care for in any other woman. It made him want her even more. Julia could make him angrier than anyone, and he loved her for it. Feelings aside, the reality was that he was better off with a woman like Renee Scales.

He began to think about Renee. He wasn't blind. He'd known she was developing feelings for him that went far beyond any he had for her. Still he hadn't acknowledged them. He hadn't told her there was no chance, and now there was this sham engagement story floating around. Sham or not, she'd be humiliated. Sure, she'd brought it on herself by perpetrating the lie in the first place, but hadn't he been doing the same thing for his own reasons? The strokes against his chest became firmer and Cortez shook his head as images of Julia filled his mind.

"I'm gonna lose him."

Correll frowned at Renee and leaned back behind his desk to watch her. "Hmph, I wondered how long it would take for you to come clean about your feelings. But a phony engagement story, Renee? That's a bit desperate, isn't it? Hasn't earned you any brownie points with my brother, that's for sure."

Renee rolled her eyes. "Well, I'm glad to know I've

got you to talk to," she said, deciding to come clean about her true feelings. She and Correll had discovered something of a kinship shortly after she and Cortez began working together as coanchors. A time or two Renee even wondered whether she'd become interested in the wrong brother. She and Correll, however, were too much alike for anything romantic to last between them. With a heavy sigh, she fixed Correll with a hard look. "Now that I've had time to be around her, I realize that I can't stand the woman. It's like she wears sex on her sleeve. She's so obvious and blatant with it."

"Yeah," Correll sighed lustily, obviously in favor of Julia's demeanor.

"It's disgusting," Renee snapped, shooting him an angry look.

Correll leaned forward and braced his fingers together on top of the polished mahogany desk. "You're taking this too hard, you know?"

Renee pointed a finger toward him. "I don't think I'm taking it hard enough. I was a fool to suggest dinner tonight, but I needed to see them together. It's obvious how much he still wants her. Any man probably would."

"Damn right," Correll wickedly replied, a wolfish grin on his handsome face.

Renee's smile was just as wicked. "I'm glad you feel that way."

"What are you cookin' up?" Correll asked, his stare filled with suspicion.

Renee re-crossed her legs and settled more comfortably in her chair. "With your help, I think I have a plan to get Julia Kelly out of Cortez's life for good."

Chapter 12

The telephone rang just as Julia and Monique prepared to step out of the hotel room.

"Damn it," Julia groaned, dropping her purse on the table and heading to the phone. "Yeah?"

"Julia? You got a minute to talk?"

Julia frowned the instant she heard Correll Wallace's voice on the line. She turned and waved Monique back inside the room. "How'd you get my number?"

"I got it from Renee so I could invite you to the party."

Julia took a seat on the arm of one of the chairs. "Party?" she asked suspiciously.

"Yeah. I have pool parties all through the summer. I wanted to throw one while you were still in town. How about it?"

Julia knew Cortez was sure to be there. The best

thing for her would be to see as little of him as possible. "Thanks, Correll, but I think I better skip this one."

"Excuse me?" Correll asked, obviously surprised that she was turning down a function his brother was sure to attend. "It's gonna be a good one, Julia. Besides a heated pool, I've got a Jacuzzi. Good people, good music. Plenty to eat and drink."

"Listen, Correll, it's probably not the greatest idea."

"Okay. Look, just stop by for a while. You won't be under pressure to stay. I just thought you could use a nice change of pace while you're here."

Julia rolled her eyes. "You got that right."

"So, can I put you on the guest list?"

"All right, I guess you can put me down." Julia accepted against her better judgment. She spent a few more moments talking to Correll about the date, time and place. When Julia hung up, she shook her head toward Monique.

"What the hell was that about?" Monique demanded.

Cortez greeted Julia with a dark frown when he opened his front door. There she stood on his front step, looking up at him with accusing eyes.

Julia prepared for Cortez to tell her to get lost. Of course, the look on his face could have done that just as effectively. Before he could speak, though, Julia raised her hand and took one final step. "I swear I didn't come here to start anything."

Cortez leaned against the doorjamb and let his chocolate gaze trail Julia's body. "You didn't come to start anything? Then that would leave you with nothing to do."

Julia nodded, accepting the jibe. "I have something I need to ask you."

"What?"

"Can I at least come in, Cork?"

Cortez watched her a moment longer. Then he muttered a dark curse and stepped away from the door.

"Are you trying to set me up with Correll?" Julia asked, as soon as they entered the sunken living room of the townhouse.

Cortez's laugh was full and loud. "I wouldn't do that to him."

Julia's smile reflected no humor. "So why'd he invite me to his party?"

Cortez shrugged and walked past her. "I've got no idea."

"I don't believe you."

"I don't care what you believe," Cortez spat. "I wouldn't do a thing to keep you around any longer than necessary."

"Don't worry, Corky. I won't be around much longer," Julia assured him.

"When are you leaving?" he asked, his back turned, trying to retain the firmness in his deep voice.

"Soon. I can't keep putting off the Haven guys," she said. "They should hear the news that I couldn't change your mind about the job ASAP." Julia waited for Cortez to turn and face her before she continued. "Anyway, I can see how happy you are with Renee. I guess I was ignoring that," she admitted. Unable to tolerate Cortez's intense stare studying her, Julia turned and headed toward the cluttered bookcase. "She really is a sweet person. I don't think I could hurt her like that, you know?" she asked, turning back to face Cortez.

His heavy, black brows arched slightly as he watched Julia. It was obvious that he was searching for the motive behind her change of heart. Unable to believe she was for real, he headed across the room until he stood before her.

Julia lowered her eyes to hide the tears shimmering there. Cortez watched her for a long while. When he saw the moisture sparkling in on the thick fringe of her lashes, he lifted her chin with his index finger.

"What are you up to this time?"

"I'm not up to anything," Julia assured him, blinking past her tears.

Cortez's wide, sensual mouth tilted upwards into a sinister smirk. It was more than obvious that he was doubtful.

"Look, I admit that I came home to mess things up between you and Renee. It was stupid and wrong of me, but it's the truth. And I'd be an even bigger fool than I already am to deny, to *keep* denying, how happy you are. You and Renee are really good together."

Cortez could not look past the sincerity in Julia's slanting, black stare. He could not believe she was standing there throwing in the towel. He was shocked that her decision fueled the need to have her in his arms.

Julia's stare faltered when she felt Cortez's finger trail from her chin across her jaw to the smooth column of her neck. The burning caress stopped at the front of her sky-blue silk blouse. She gasped when Cortez leaned forward and nibbled the satiny smooth skin beneath her ear.

"Cortez, what are you doing?"

"I don't believe you're giving up so easily. It's not your style," he whispered, as his lips sucked the diamond stud in her earlobe. Meanwhile, his massive hands explored her full breasts. The nipples instantly hardened and pressed against the delicate silk.

Julia's gasp resembled a soft hiccup. She ordered herself

to remain impassive, trying to ignore the coaxing thumbs caressing the firm tips of her breasts.

"Fighting hasn't gotten me anywhere," she managed to reply.

"So you're just gonna let me go on with my life?" Cortez asked, sliding one long, perfectly toned arm around her waist and pulling her closer. His hand delved beneath her short-sleeved blouse and stroked her bare skin.

Julia opened her mouth to respond, but Cortez's merciless taunting prevented that. All she could manage was a jerky nod.

Cortez pulled his hand from her chest and cupped her neck. He forced her head before his lips fell upon hers. His tongue nuzzled the dark interior of her mouth. They groaned in unison and the kiss deepened. Their tongues fought passionately as their hands sought to memorize every inch of each other's bodies.

The strength of Cortez's embrace mixed with the force of his kiss could have been frightening. For Julia, it was intoxicating. How long had she dreamed of them this way?

When Cortez cupped her buttocks and lifted her against him, Julia came back to reality. Knowing what motivated his kiss caused her to pull away.

Cortez was more than a little shocked to feel Julia withdrawing from him. For a few long moments, only the sound of heavy breathing could be heard.

"Did I pass your test?" she finally asked, without looking into his eyes.

Cortez was obviously unable to answer. He simply watched Julia until she retrieved her purse from his sofa and left.

Chapter 13

"You don't have to be so excited, Daddy. It's not like I won the lottery or anything."

Darius Kelly's intriguing dark eyes twinkled as he watched his youngest daughter. "Julia, baby, it's almost as good. With that boy out of your life, you can start giving some of those other poor souls a chance," the retired police detective drawled.

Julia laughed and tossed a packet of crackers at her father. They were having lunch the next afternoon when Julia informed her father that she was through with Cortez. Of course, Darius Kelly couldn't have been more pleased.

"I think I'm gonna take a break from men for a while," Julia sighed, smoothing her hands across the satin sleeves of her orange dress.

Darius frowned. "Take a break from men?"

"Daddy," Julia called in a warning tone, about to bubble

over with laughter again. "*From relationships.* I promise you I don't wanna explore any other romantic avenues," she assured her father in the frank manner he always urged from her and her sister.

"Whew, thank God," Darius sighed, running a hand over his salt-and-pepper Afro. "I tell ya', girl, a man my age can't take an upset like that. I'm goin' to the men's room."

"Okay." Julia laughed. Why couldn't men be more like her father? Not only was he handsome, but he had a great sense of humor and he didn't play games. Shrugging, Julia admitted that she was glad she had given up the chase too. Maybe now she could concentrate on finding a man like that. More important, maybe she and Cortez could concentrate on being friends.

Julia looked up and saw that Correll Wallace was standing over her. "Hey, how long have you been here?" she asked, smiling.

"A while," Correll told her, stroking the smooth line of his jaw. "You look like you're in deep thought about something."

"Yeah."

"So are you ready for the party?" Correll asked, taking a seat at the table.

Julia nodded. "I could use a party right about now."

Correll leaned forward, a frown on his handsome face. "Hey, you all right? You seem kind of down." he asked, patting her hand.

"You better not cancel your party because of it," Julia teased, managing a smile. Her light mood faded when she saw Cortez across the dining room.

Correll noticed the direction of her gaze and turned. "We're having lunch together," he informed Julia while waving at his brother.

"You better not keep him waiting, then," Julia softly advised.

Correll stood and was about to press a kiss to Julia's cheek. He heard someone clearing his throat next to him and looked up. "Hey, Mr. Kelly," he politely greeted Julia's father.

"Correll," Darius replied unaffectedly, taking his seat.

Correll accepted the cool dismissal and left the table.

"What was that about?" Cortez asked his brother as soon as they had taken their seats.

"What?" Correll asked, studying his menu.

Cortez scratched the soft baby hair near his temple. "You and Julia?"

"Why are you so interested?"

Cortez grimaced and lifted his menu. "I'm not. I did notice how close you seemed at dinner, though."

Correll pushed his menu aside and leaned back in his chair. "What are you trying to say, Tez?"

"I'm just making an observation."

"What's that supposed to mean?"

Cortez was silent for a while. Then he looked up at Correll and shrugged. "She came to the house yesterday and said she was giving up on me."

"What?"

"I know. That's what I said. She told me about how nice Renee was and how she just couldn't hurt her like that."

"Hmph." Correll gestured, just as confused as Cortez was. "What do you make of it?" he asked, watching his brother shrug. "You don't think she'd start playin' hard to get now or act like she doesn't care to get you interested, do you?"

Cortez didn't answer. At the moment, he hadn't a clue of what Julia wanted.

* * *

The neatly manicured lawn surrounding Correll Wallace's home was filled with cars. Correll's parties were a staple of the summer, and they were always successful. This one was no exception. People could be found in almost every area of the house and lawn. There was an abundance of laughter, talking and dancing, and the guests helped themselves to the impressive bar and buffet.

Julia decided to park her rental car across the street and walk over to the house. It took quite a while to make her way inside, with old friends she hadn't seen in a while wanting to talk to her. After about fifteen minutes she found Correll. He was standing amidst a small group gathered around the grill. When Julia tapped Correll's shoulder, he turned and smiled.

"Girl, I'm glad you made it!" he exclaimed, pulled her close for a hug. After a moment, he stood back to look at her. His hazel stare slowly traveled over her stylish turquoise bikini top and the very short cutoffs she wore. "I'm glad you made it."

Julia laughed. "You already said that."

"That's because I really, really mean it."

Julia's lovely midnight gaze faltered briefly. The longer she talked with Correll, the more obvious it became that the handsome advertising entrepreneur was determined to keep her by his side all night. Still, despite Correll's overt advances, Julia had a very nice time. She felt really good about deciding to come to the party. That is, until Cortez arrived with his fiancée.

"Hey, how about checkin' out my heated pool," Correll whispered in Julia's ear. His arms slid around her waist as he led her out of the dining room.

Cortez grumbled about finding Correll even as he scanned the crowded living room. It didn't take long for him to spot his older brother with Julia. When he saw how cozy they looked, his jaw tightened. The tiny muscle there danced erratically, but Cortez decided not to interrupt.

Renee's gaze followed Cortez's, and she saw Julia and Correll, as well. It was clear that Cortez was not happy, and she grimaced.

"I think the heated pool is a good idea," Julia said. She was so preoccupied with Cortez she couldn't concentrate on Correll's traveling hands.

Smiling, Correll stopped and turned Julia in his arms. "I think it's just what you need," he decided, massaging her bare shoulders. "Damn, you're tense as hell. What's wrong?"

Julia's smile didn't quite reach her eyes. She just stared over Correll's shoulder.

"Well, there he is. Let's go say hello," Renee suggested, pulling Cortez along behind her.

"We shouldn't interrupt," Cortez told Renee, watching his brother lead Julia out of the dining room.

Renee sighed and toyed with a lock of her hair dangling from her ponytail. "Cortez, it's a party. I'm sure he'd want to know you're here."

Cortez fanned the forest green T-shirt he wore away from his chest. "Later," he grumbled, heading over to the bar for a chilled beer.

"I never did thank you for inviting me to tag along," Renee said in a voice of phony appreciation. Clearly, her presence there was only for Julia Kelly's benefit.

Cortez twisted the cap off an icy beer bottle and took a long swallow. "Not a problem."

"Cortez, why don't you tell me what the problem is so we can at least *try* to have a good time?"

He fixed her with a blank stare. "What problem?"

"I don't know…" Renee trailed away innocently.

"Fine. Let's go," Cortez hurriedly announced and headed in the direction he had seen Correll and Julia take.

"Cortez, we don't have to."

"Nah, Renee. You won't be happy unless I see Correll, so let's go."

Renee watched Cortez walk out before her. Her innocent expression turned into a cunning one.

"What's up, man?" Cortez greeted his brother and managed a slight smirk for good measure. He stood over the pool with one hand pushed into his sagging blue jean shorts. That hand was clenched into a fist, turning his palm a deep shade of crimson. Correll, who was already lounging back in the pool with his arm resting on the ledge behind Julia, looked up in surprise. "Hey, man, glad you made it! Hop in!"

"Nah," Cortez declined, his smoky stare trained on Julia's dark form glistening in the water. "Too hot for me in there."

Julia tried to maintain eye contact with Cortez but it was near impossible. She wanted him so much. Accepting that he could have cared less, no matter what she did, was killing her.

Cortez was fighting just as hard to keep his composure. Seeing Julia next to his brother ate away at him. Blinded by jealousy, he didn't fully register that Julia wasn't exactly *snuggled* next to Correll. In fact, she was actually standing while Correll lounged back. That detail went unnoticed by Cortez, unfortunately.

"You could throw one of these things every week and people would be here," Renee was telling Correll. They had been talking while Cortez and Julia tried to ignore each other.

Correll laughed. "You know, Renee, that's a good idea. What do you think, man?"

"I need another drink," Cortez grumbled. He tilted his beer bottle to his mouth and walked away.

Julia's eyes followed Cortez so intently that she actually turned in the pool.

"Something wrong, Julia?" Renee asked, her brow rising slightly.

Julia shook her head quickly and resumed a more relaxing position in the pool. "You better go check on him."

Renee nodded, giving Correll a sharp glance. "My fiancé hasn't been in a good mood all day," she informed them before leaving.

It was hard to miss the sadness on Julia's face. "Hey," Correll softly called, cupping Julia's chin in his palm. "It's not that bad."

Julia managed a nod, but her exquisite dark stare lowered once more. A gasp escaped her lips the next minute when Correll kissed her.

"Correll! What are you doing?" she demanded, pushing herself away from him.

"I'm trying to help."

Julia smiled at the simple admission. "It's not necessary. And why are you being so helpful all of a sudden, especially when you never gave a damn about me before?" Her eyes narrowed in further suspicion. "Or is this all because your brother and I are done and you're hoping for a turn?"

Correll smoothed a wet hand across his neck and had the decency to appear remorseful. "I'm sorry, Julia. For everything. Cortez told me about what you overheard, what I said that night. Truth be told, I never had anything against you. But Ma...she has *ideas* about the sort of women her sons should take to the altar."

"And their beds," Julia noted.

"That, too." Correll chuckled. "I admit to buying into her anger and overreacting that night. I guess that proves I care more about the family name than I thought."

Though Julia continued to watch him curiously, she couldn't dismiss the fact that she thought he was being sincere. Without another word, she left Correll alone in the pool and missed the cunning intensity return to his gaze.

Correll spent another ten minutes relaxing in the heated water after Julia's departure. He was about to go looking for her when Renee appeared.

"Where is she?"

Correll didn't bother to look at Renee as he reached for a towel. "Who?"

Renee rolled her eyes toward the sky and sighed. "You know who. Julia."

"She left."

"Why?"

"I kissed her. She left."

Renee gave him a dry look. "That's not the reaction I would have expected."

"Me, neither."

"What is wrong with you?" Renee furiously whispered. Propping her hands over the black-and-gray silk wrap around her waist, she stormed over to Correll. "I want this taken care of. Fast."

Correll's smile was lazy and confident. "I have it all under control."

Julia had hidden herself away in an unoccupied area off of the kitchen. She sat there sipping on a creamy mixed drink and berating herself. *God, what was I thinking?* she silently moaned. Attending that party, thinking she had a chance with Cortez…This had to be the biggest mistake she'd ever made. The thing was she couldn't seem to stop it. Again, she'd opened her heart to Cortez, and again she had come out a loser.

Shaking her head, Julia decided to forget it all and start over. Standing, she took another sip of her drink and turned to head back into the party. Unfortunately, Cortez was blocking her way.

"Excuse me," Julia mumbled, figuring she would walk around him.

Cortez brushed her arm and tugged her close. "What are you doing with Correll?" His voice was soft but probing.

Julia, shocked by the question, stood there watching him with an open mouth. Was that jealousy she saw in his eyes? "It's none of your business," she slowly replied, trying to extract her arm from his now iron grip.

The look on Cortez's face gradually took on the appearance of a frown. His temper weakened and he pulled Julia with him into the pantry and snapped on the dim light that hung overhead. "Don't play this game, Julia," he urged, trapping her against the door.

"Games? No, Cork, that would be you."

Cortez shook his head. The look in his eyes spoke volumes.

"Why won't you just tell me the truth about what's going on?"

Cortez's stare raked Julia's scantily clad body warmly before turning cold. Giving her a stony glare, he pulled her away from the door. "Not knowing doesn't feel so good, does it?" he whispered, leaving the pantry.

She watched him leave, her vision blurred by tears.

* * *

Julia was on her way to the nearest exit. She took off into a light sprint following the talk with Cortez.

"Hey, where're you goin'?"

Julia closed her eyes briefly, before she turned and smiled. "I gotta get out of here. Now."

Correll tilted his head and watched her closely. "What's going on? I thought I had you out of this mood."

Julia focused on her key ring. "I've just had enough socializing for one day," she said, tracing the bronze letters of the ring, which spelled out her name.

"Well, the party's starting to thin out. Why don't you stay? I hate for people to leave my parties upset."

A brief but genuine smile crossed Julia's full lips. "I'm not upset, just—"

Correll smoothed his hand along her baby-soft bare arm. "Look, you can't let whatever it is rule your emotions like this. Not anymore. You'll be a mess."

Julia took a deep breath. "How sad it is that I'm too much of an idiot to realize that."

"Does this mean you'll stay?"

"I guess for a little while." Julia nodded eventually. She took the arm Correll offered and let him lead her deeper into the house.

Cortez found his brother ten minutes later. "Hey, man. Wait up," he called.

Correll was out dumping large troughs of oil that had been used for frying fish. "What?" he called, pouring a tub of the grease into a deep hole dug behind one of the huge trees at the edge of his backyard.

"I need to talk to you."

Correll gave his brother a completely innocent look.

"Man, look, if this is about me and Julia in the pool, we're just friends."

Cortez shook his head. "Yeah, it's about Julia, but not about that."

"What then?"

Cortez stroked his bearded cheek. "Listen, I'll probably call you after I take Renee home, all right?"

Correll just nodded as he watched his brother leave. A look of concern clouded his face.

The party was completely over about an hour and a half later. Julia waited for Correll to bid the last guest goodbye before she stepped forward.

"You're pretty good at these parties." She complimented him after the last two guests walked out the door. "I had a very nice time."

Correll closed the double mahogany doors and leaned against them. "Thanks, but they wear me out. You're not leaving, are you?" he asked, his eyes staring at her purse.

Julia held her arms out at her sides. "Well, the party *is* over."

"I'm not cool about your state of mind yet."

"What? Correll, I'm fine. There was nothing for you to worry about. I was just feeling sorry for myself."

Correll pushed himself from the door and grabbed her hand. "Well, have one more drink with me before you go."

"One drink and then I have to leave, Correll. I mean it," Julia decided, dropping her purse and key ring onto an end table.

Correll nodded absently as he prepared the drinks. He made them both Long Island iced teas, but in Julia's he put an extra dose of each liquor in the drink. "So what was wrong with you today?" he asked, handing Julia her drink.

"I'm wising up."

"What's that supposed to mean?" Correll asked, sipping his drink.

Julia smoothed her hand across her short hair and groaned. "I did come here to agitate things with Cortez and his fiancée."

Correll's face responded in surprise. "You sure you wanna be tellin' me this?"

Julia sipped from her glass and savored the slight sting of the drink. "Well, I already told Cortez, so—"

"What'd he say?" Correll asked, watching Julia closely as she drank deeply from her tall glass.

"He doesn't believe me."

"Should he?"

Julia stood and walked over to the black baby grand piano in the center of the room. "Yeah, he should. I meant it."

"Just like that?"

"Yes."

"So, what now?"

Julia shrugged and tipped the rest of the burgundy-colored liquid down her throat. "Look, I admit I was wrong. Right up until he stormed out of the restaurant that night I thought he was just trying to ignore me so his feelings would go away and he'd try to be happy. Then I realized that maybe he really was happy. It just hit me out of nowhere…" Julia trailed away and noticed Correll watching her intently. "Am I surprising you?"

"Hell, yeah," Correll admitted. He couldn't believe what he was hearing.

Julia yawned, stretching her arms overhead. "Well, I've been doing a lot of that lately…." She squeezed her eyes tight against the heaviness weighing down her eyelids. "Correll, I think I better get going while I can still keep my eyes open." The moment she turned from the piano she felt dizzy. "Uh-oh," she whispered, leaning back against the baby grand.

Correll was by her side in a flash. "You okay?" he asked softly, his thumbs brushing the undersides of her breasts.

"I must be more tired than I thought."

"You want to sit down for a minute?"

Julia shook her head, wincing slightly at the light in the room. "I'll be fine. It won't take long to get to my hotel," she assured Correll, turning to head out of the living room. She had only taken a few steps when the dizziness overwhelmed her.

"Whoa," Correll called, catching Julia's light form in his arms. "You should lie down," he said, carrying her upstairs to his bedroom.

"No, Correll." Julia weakly resisted as she tried to squirm out of his arms.

"Julia, stop," Correll softly ordered, his hands tightening slightly against her bare skin. "You just need to lie down for a little while, all right?"

She was already succumbing to the effects of sudden weariness and ceased her resistance. "All right. Just for a little while."

Chapter 14

Cortez leaned back against the headrest in his truck and sighed. He'd just dropped Renee off at her home and at last acknowledged his real frustration. When Julia left all those years ago, he insisted, to himself and everyone else, that they just weren't right for one another. He knew he'd been fooling himself. Her forceful, demanding and sexually confident nature had always put him on edge. It was that *edge* that made the arousal for her so damn irresistible, a reason why he never forced the issue about her not wanting to marry. For such a long time that arousal had been more than enough. He'd never realized how much it overwhelmed what should have been the far more important and stronger aspects of their relationship. Additionally, he hadn't realized how much that *edge* overshadowed the ugliness she'd experienced with his family.

Ever since he'd seen her in Los Angeles there'd been a

gnawing at his will. Now, for some reason, she intrigued him far more than she ever had. This time there was more, and for the life of him he couldn't put his finger on what it was.

"Yeah, she's got her sights set on my brother," he said aloud in the dark interior of his sport utility vehicle. He wouldn't let himself accept that something in that statement didn't ring quite true.

Cortez shook his head as he rubbed one hand over his soft, wavy hair. He really needed to talk to someone. Picking up the phone resting in front of the gearshift, he decided to call his brother. He had punched in the first three digits and then decided to stop by Correll's house instead.

"Oh…my head…and everything else…" Julia groaned, pushing her hands through her short, dark locks.

The dizziness hadn't let up very much, but she managed to push herself into a sitting position. She noticed two things: First, she was in a strange bed. Second, she was totally nude!

As she was far too groggy to do anything about the situation, she gave in to it. Falling back to the bed, she moaned.

Correll was downstairs at the bar pouring two glasses of champagne. Glancing back over his shoulder at the staircase, he shook his head. He had decided to take more time with his plan. Though once he had gotten Julia out of her clothes, he knew he wouldn't be able to resist a taste of the sweet, dark beauty for long.

Placing the bottle of Dom Perignon back in the small refrigerator he began to make his way out of the living room. The front doorbell rang just as he stepped from around the bar. Frowning, he looked out through window and saw his brother's truck.

"Damn," he muttered, hoping Cortez wasn't in the mood for a lengthy visit. He wanted to be there when she awakened. Hopefully the extra liquor he'd slipped into her drink would have her far too relaxed to resist letting nature take its course. He'd thought of sleeping with her since the first time Cortez had introduced them. Being so close now, he wasn't about to let a thing interfere with the conquest.

The rings of the bell became longer and more insistent. Correll didn't want them to awaken Julia, so he went on and opened the door to his brother.

The fierce frown on Cortez's caramel-toned face deepened when the door finally opened. "What took you so long?"

"What's up, man?" Correll greeted him uneasily.

"I need to talk." Cortez sighed, rubbing a hand across his whiskered jaw as he walked inside. When he turned and saw the two glasses and Correll in his boxer shorts, he groaned. "Sorry, man."

Correll simply shrugged and looked away. Instantly, Cortez had a bad feeling about what he'd walked in on. Turning away from his brother, he walked farther into the house.

"I dropped Renee off at her house and drove around for a while. I needed to talk to you," Cortez absently explained. His gaze was intense while he inspected the living room.

"Well, man, you can call me tomorrow. We can have lunch or something."

Of course, Correll's obvious attempt at getting his little brother to leave did not work. If anything, Cortez was even more suspicious. He was about to leave the living room when his eyes fell to the bronze key ring on the end table. A host of keys dangled from the ring bearing Julia's name.

Cortez turned and looked up toward the ceiling. Then he stormed up the carpeted stairway.

"Tez!" Correll bellowed, rushing up the stairs behind his brother. His heart pounded frantically, as the champagne sloshed outside the glasses he was still holding. "Cortez!"

Julia was moving restlessly against the sheets. Far off she could hear shouting and heavy footsteps. Still very disoriented, she threw back the covers and tried to make her way out of the bed. Unfortunately, she only fell to her back.

Cortez halted in front of the closed bedroom door and closed his eyes. He prayed silently for his suspicions to be unfounded. Pushing against the door, he opened his eyes.

As he suspected, there in his brother's bed was Julia. Her lovely features were relaxed as she slept peacefully. Cortez's mouth opened as his sluggish steps brought him closer to the bed. He rubbed his hands through his hair as his eyes traced Julia's flawless, dark body. He couldn't stop himself from trying to memorize every inch of it. Despite the circumstances, he felt himself respond to the sight of her.

Correll cleared his throat. "Cortez, man—"

Cortez simply raised his hand, not wanting to hear anything his brother had to say.

After a while, Julia's eyes fluttered open and she saw Cortez looming above her. "Cork," she sighed, a lazy smile crossing her full lips.

The sound of her voice shook Cortez from his trancelike state. He bent down and took her arms in an unbreakable hold.

The stinging force of the grip forced a moan from Julia. "Cortez," She whispered.

"Shut up!" Cortez ordered, as he shook her fiercely.

"Cortez," Julia groaned, a bit louder this time. Though she was still groggy, she recognized the voice that yelled at her.

The terrible accusations Cortez hurled at her caused her head to spin again. Looking past the murderous expression on his face, Julia saw Correll standing across the room with two glasses. Everything fell into place when she saw that he was in his boxers. "Cortez, please…" she whispered again.

Cortez fixed her with a scathing look and pushed her back to the bed. "You are truly something else," he whispered.

Julia held out a hand in a defensive gesture. "Cortez, please. I swear I don't know what this is. I don't know what's going on…please."

Cortez's handsome face was darkened by the look of pure disgust he gave Julia. With a hateful smirk, he shook his head and left the room.

Julia pulled the sheet off the bed and wrapped it around her body. She ran after Cortez, tears streaming down her lovely face. "Cortez! Cortez, wait!" she called, hurrying down the stairs after him. From the corner of her eye, she noticed Correll following along.

"Cortez! Don't go! Please let me try to explain this!" Julia cried, wiping her face with the back of her hand. She caught Cortez just as he reached the last step. "Cortez, wait." She pleaded, grabbing the edge of his jeans by a back pocket.

Cortez was so blinded by anger he could barely breathe. When he felt Julia touch him he turned with undiluted rage filtering his smoky eyes.

Julia's onyx gaze was trained on the hate she saw on the face of the man she loved. She pressed her fingers against her mouth and watched Cortez pull away. He left her with a long glare before leaving the house.

When the door slammed behind Cortez Julia fell to her knees. Correll closed his eyes and tried to tune out her loud wailing. His ultimate goal to turn Cortez against Julia had been fulfilled. Unfortunately, seeing Julia broken and crying hysterically made him sick inside. He cursed himself for ever taking part in such a cruel scheme.

"Julia? Julia, come on, honey. Let's get up," he gently persuaded. "Let's go back to bed."

Although Julia was in shock, Correll's words sobered her. "What happened here?" she asked, pulling away from him.

Correll knew he had done a terrible thing, but he couldn't admit that to Julia. "We slept together," he lied, watching the confusion in her eyes fade into hopelessness. Like a limp doll, she dragged herself back upstairs to get dressed.

"What happened to you?" Renee asked Cortez, when he opened his door early the next morning. She was shocked to see him looking so drained. "I've been trying to call you since you dropped me off last night."

Cortez moved away from the door so Renee could enter. "I got in late," he grumbled, rubbing his firm stomach in an absent manner.

"What's wrong with you?"

"I don't feel like talkin' about it."

"Cortez—"

"Renee, please, all right?"

Renee walked over to him. Taking hold of his arm, she made him face her. "What is going on with you? You answer the door looking like hell and you tell me nothing's wrong?"

Cortez jerked away from Renee, his expression murderous. "What the hell do you expect? It's eight-thirty in the damn morning!"

"It's not like you to miss a budget meeting at the station. I wanted to come check on you after we tried calling and got no answer," Renee quietly explained.

Cortez walked through the house to the kitchen. He poured himself a glass of orange juice and then looked at her. "I had a fight with Correll last night."

"Over Julia?" Renee blurted.

"What?" Cortez asked, a small furrow forming between his thick brows.

"You just looked very, um, aggravated when they were at the party together." Renee sighed, covering her slip.

"Right," Cortez muttered, taking a sip of the juice.

Renee managed to hide her smile at Cortez's cold words. "When are you gonna talk to Correll?"

"I'm not."

"Excuse me?"

Cortez finished his juice and slammed the glass onto the counter. "I don't really have anything else to say to him."

"Cortez, baby, you can't let whatever happened come between you two."

Cortez lifted one toned shoulder in a lazy shrug. "It's too late for that. I don't want to see him again."

Renee's laugh was short and humorless. "How can you turn your back on your own brother? Unless there's more going on with you and Julia?"

"Drop it, Renee," Cortez ordered, squeezing his eyes shut. The last thing he wanted was to think of his feelings for Julia Kelly.

Renee decided to heed Cortez's warning. She hoped she could convince Correll to set things right, so this would work to both their advantages.

"I'll see you at the station later, all right?" she called, making a mad dash out of the house.

"Damn it, Lila, didn't I ask you to do this yesterday?" Correll snapped at his secretary, who just watched him with stunned eyes.

Lila Harris ordered herself not to snap back at her usually wonderful boss. "I did take care of it, Correll. These are just the copies you asked me to make."

Correll gave the papers a closer look, closing his eyes in regret. "I'm sorry," he mumbled.

Lila rolled her eyes and turned away from the desk, walking past Renee, who had just witnessed the scene.

"Hey, can I talk to you?"

Correll groaned when he saw Renee in his office. "This isn't the day," he warned her.

"What happened?"

Correll sighed, remembering the previous night. "I planned on helping Julia pass out and then I would convince her we had slept together. I'd insist on telling Cortez, knowing she'd leave before letting him find out."

"But?"

"But Cortez paid a surprise visit to my house. He found Julia in my bed. It wasn't pretty after that."

"My God." Renee breathed, taking a seat before the large desk in the corner of the room. "I can't believe you did that. You really need to talk to Cortez before more time passes and things get even more out of hand," she advised.

"I don't think that's a good idea," Correll decided.

"Honey, Cortez told me he never wants to see you again."

Correll's intense hazel stare snapped to Renee's face. "I'm not gonna lose my brother over this crap. I mean that."

A suspicious frown darkened Renee's honey-toned face. "What's that supposed to mean?"

Correll stood behind his desk. "That means I'm tellin' Cortez about this whole foolish mess."

"You can't!" Renee ordered, her large eyes following him around the office. "Please, Correll."

"Renee, you just told me my brother may not want to talk to me again. You expect me to just sit by and let that happen?"

Renee took a deep breath. "Now, listen to me. Cortez isn't going to stay mad over this. You are his brother. He'll forgive you in time. It's Julia he's really angry with. I'm sure she'll be heading back to Los Angeles by the end of the day."

Correll sighed and sat back down. He covered his face in his hands and groaned.

Julia smoothed her hands across her flaring mocha-colored skirt, which reached just above her knee. She waited patiently for Cortez to open his door. She didn't know what could possibly be said, but she had to try.

The door flew open and Cortez stood there with a murderous glare on his face. If possible, that glare deepened when he saw that Julia was his unexpected guest.

"Can I come in?" she asked, glad that he hadn't slammed the door in her face immediately.

Cortez stepped aside to allow her in. "You got a lot of nerve comin' up in here when I'm so close to..." The growling threat trailed away as he slammed the front door once she'd entered.

Julia's heart flew to her chest at the sincerity of his words. "Why are you so upset over this?"

"What?" Cortez whispered. He tilted his head slightly, certain he had misunderstood her.

"You're so upset over this. Why? You've told me time and time again that you're not interested in me, in us, again."

Cortez watched Julia unblinkingly. It was obvious by the look in his eyes that he did not believe what he was hearing. "So that makes it all right for you to sleep with my brother then? Is that what you're telling me?"

Julia closed her eyes. She tried to steel herself against the effect that his slightly raspy, deep voice had on her. "Cortez—"

"Does that make it all right?"

"No, but..." Julia's uneasy words trailed away.

As she struggled to find the right way to explain things, Cortez lost his patience. He bounded across the living room.

Julia backed away from him. "Cortez wait, please—"

"Don't!" he roared, his intense stare faltered while he fought to maintain a grip on his temper.

Julia pressed her lips together, her vision blurred by tears. "Cortez, please. I don't remember what happened," she said, watching Cortez's hateful glare narrow. "I don't know if I slept with Correll or not."

"Right," Cortez snarled, continuing his trek toward her.

"Cortez, wait! I'm trying to explain this!" Julia hated to beg, but she was racking her brain for the right words to soothe his raging temper.

Unfortunately, her pleas fell on deaf ears. Cortez did not stop until he caught Julia. One of his large hands grasped her upper arm, and he set her back against the wall. Closing his eyes, he prayed for the strength to fend off the rage that seemed to be blinding him.

Finally, out of breath and weary, Cortez pressed his forehead against Julia's and took several gulps of air. Her slender form trembled against him as she, too, tried to catch her breath. In the midst of it all, their lips met. Soon, they were caught in a kiss of desperation and desire. Cortez thrust his tongue deep into Julia's mouth. She moaned, mimicking the action, as she felt his hands roaming her body feverishly.

Moments later, his large hands were beneath her. They squeezed her thighs mercilessly. He broke the kiss, pressing hot, wet licks down the length of her neck. Taking Julia by the hips, he positioned her straddling one of his muscular thighs.

With unwavering intent, his hands caressed her body possessively. Finding their way beneath her skirt once more, he pulled at the flimsy underpants she wore, succeeding in ripping them away.

"Cortez…" Julia moaned when she felt his fingers plunge into her. Unashamedly, she moved against him while he caressed the part of her body that cried out for his attention. "Please make love to me," she whispered, stroking his rough jaw.

The words stilled Cortez's fingers and he pulled away. Once again, his expression was cold. "Get out," he ordered, his voice hollow, defeated.

Julia dried her eyes. She was hurt and, for the second

time in her life, felt ashamed. Picking up her underwear that lay ripped on the floor, she stuffed them into her purse. Without looking back, she left the house. She swore this was the last time she would let Cortez Wallace turn her world inside out.

Chapter 15

Several weeks passed after the terrible fight. In that time Cortez had become more involved in his work. His personal life, however, was suffering greatly. He had made quick work of dispelling any and all rumors of his supposed engagement to Renee Scales. He realized that whatever had or hadn't happened between Correll and Julia didn't matter. He was suddenly overcome by an urge to look in the mirror—needing to verify that it was he who had indeed fallen for Julia once again. He loved and wanted her more than he ever had before.

Like an idiot, he'd screwed up royally. This time, however, he feared the situation couldn't be undone. He knew she had every right to hate him. Sadly, that acknowledgement did nothing to diminish how brutally his actions were tearing him up inside.

"Hello. This is Lexi."

"I'm sorry, Lexi," Cortez said. "This is Cortez Wallace.

I must've misdialed. Thought I was getting Julia's private line."

"Oh, hello, Mr. Wallace. No need to apologize. You've got the right number." Lexi cleared her throat, inserting Cortez's name for Julia, who was leaning on the corner of the desk.

Julia set aside the demographics report she'd been viewing. When Lexi raised her hand in question, Julia shook her head no.

"Uh…" Lexi cleared her throat to mask sudden unease. "Julia's in a meeting just now, I'm afraid."

"Would you tell her I called, Lexi?"

"Sure." Lexi couldn't mask the sympathy in her voice. She waited until the connection broke before returning the receiver to its cradle. "I could never ignore a call from a man like that," she practically moaned, eyelashes fluttering about her eyes in a dramatic fashion.

Julia barely tuned in to her assistant's words. She'd moved from her desk and was staring blankly past the tall windows lining her office.

"All right, we can do that. So I'll see you tomorrow at two for lunch?" Correll nodded, jotting the appointment in his personal calendar. When he looked up and saw Cortez in his doorway, his eyes widened. "Okay, Barry, I've got to go, but I'll see you tomorrow." He hung up and turned to Cortez. "Hey, man, what's up?" He greeted his brother as though things had not been strained between them for weeks.

"All these years you acted like you hated Julia as much as Ma," Cortez began, slamming the office door behind him. "Then, in a few hours you have her in your bed. Why?"

"Cortez—"

"The truth, Correll. Just the truth."

Correll ran one hand across his face and groaned. Cortez's request was all it took for Correll, who had wanted to be honest about this for a long time, to open up. "Listen, I got Julia to stay after the party for a drink. She wasn't up to it, but she agreed. I, um, gave her a pretty strong drink and she passed out. I put her to bed, and that's when you showed up."

Cortez shook his head slightly. "What? Were you expecting me?"

"No," Correll assured him, standing behind the desk. "The plan was to make Julia believe we'd slept together. When I got her naked…" he couldn't help but recall the look of the dark beauty pliant in his bed. He cleared his throat at the murderous intent in his brother's gaze and continued. "Once she was in my bed, the plan was to actually sleep with her. At any rate, she was so out of it that I'd planned to tell her we slept together and that I had to come clean with you. She'd leave town before something like that came out."

Cortez pushed his hands into the deep pockets of his tan trousers. He began to pace the room, trying to grasp what he was discovering. "So you did all this just to make sure I'd marry Renee? I knew you liked her, man, but Jesus."

Correll raised his hand. "No, Tez. *Renee* thought of this to make sure you'd marry her. And like a damn fool I went along."

As Correll recounted the entire story, he told his brother about Renee's concerns and her fear of Julia. When he finished Cortez was too furious to speak. When he thought of all the things he'd said and done to Julia he became nauseous.

Correll watched as his younger brother rushed to the

bathroom in the office. He could hear violent heaves as Cortez became sick. Correll didn't bother to explain any further. He knew it would be a very long time before Cortez would want to hear anything from him.

When Cortez finished in the bathroom he left without a word to his brother.

"Renee Scales's office."

"Hey, Marsha, is Renee around?"

"Oh, hi, Cortez. No, she's not."

"When are you expecting her?"

"Um, not for a while," Marsha said, as she checked the calendar on her desk. "Oh, wait up. She went over to your mom's house."

Cortez gripped the steering wheel tightly and rolled his eyes.

"Cortez? You still there?"

"Yeah, yeah, thanks, Marsha," he said before shutting off the phone. His mother's house was the last place he wanted to have this conversation. Unfortunately, this was something that could not wait.

"I want to know how something that should have been wonderful could turn out so horribly."

Renee smiled, accepting the glass of tea Cora offered. "I should never have tried to trick him. He's way too smart for that." She shrugged. "I knew that, but I tried anyway."

Cora was frowning. "You're good for my son. There has to be a way to get him to see that. Especially now, with Miss Julia Kelly finally out of the way."

The front door slammed, bringing a halt to the conversation. A few moments later Cortez appeared in the living room.

"Cortez, what a nice surprise," Cora greeted him.

"Hey, Ma," Cortez replied absently. His stare was trained on Renee.

"What's wrong?" Cora asked, laying her hand on his arm.

"I need to talk to Renee. Can you give us a few minutes?" Cortez asked, looking down at his mother.

"Sure," Cora agreed, nodding quickly. She sent Renee an uneasy look before leaving the room.

"Are you okay?" Renee asked once they were alone. Walking over to Cortez, she curved her hands about his arm.

The instant Renee touched him, Cortez moved away. He walked past her, unable to look into her eyes.

"What's wrong?"

"How could you do that to Julia?"

Realization dawned in Renee's eyes, but she quickly masked it. "Julia? Do what to Julia?"

Cortez shook his head and turned to face her. "Were you really that threatened by the woman?"

Renee's long, arched brows rose in an effort to maintain her innocence. "Cortez, honey, you're really confusing me—"

"Damn it, Renee, just admit it!"

"All right! Well, listen, Cortez, I'm not blind," she snapped, her anger spewing forth. "I could see how you drooled over that bitch every time she walked into the room."

"And that upset you because of what? Our *engagement?*"

Renee waved her hand. "And that should've showed you the kind of woman she was. Julia Kelly would've done anything to break us up."

"Except that there was nothing to break up." Cortez

cursed himself for letting the situation grow so completely out of hand. "She came to me on the day of the party to say she wasn't going to interfere."

"And you're blind if you believed that," Renee spat.

"Do you have any idea how I treated her?"

Renee rolled her eyes. "I'm sure the slut was used to it."

Cortez's eyes narrowed as he watched the woman he thought he knew. "I can't believe I'm hearing this crap from you."

"Oh, please, Cortez! Your mother told me all about Miss Julia. How sneaky and whoreish she is. I had to do something before—"

"I love her."

Renee uttered a short, cold laugh. "I had to do something before *that* happened."

"Why? Because of some deluded idea you had that there was a marriage in our future?" Cortez leaned against the back of the couch and dropped his head. "We work together, Renee. I've loved Julia since I met her. Like a fool, I convinced myself that she wasn't right for me until I believed it was true. I played along with this con of an engagement because I hoped it'd get her to leave and save me from having to deal with issues I didn't want to face."

Slowly, Renee walked toward him. "There'd be no *issues* with us, Cortez. Your relationship with Julia has been one drama fest after another. Aren't you sick of that?"

"Renee—"

"Cortez, we're good for each other. You know that." She arched herself against his chest. "We work well together. And can you imagine how successful we'd be in the bedroom?"

Cortez cupped Renee's chin and made her look up at him. "We're not right for each other. If you loved me and believed there could be something between us you never would've done this. If I felt anything more for you than a platonic friendship stemming from our work then nothing Julia said or did would've mattered to me."

The soft, pleading look in Renee's eyes hardened and she pushed herself away from Cortez. "Son of a bitch," she sneered, turning away from him.

Cortez took a deep breath and stood. Regardless of what happened, he didn't want to end things harshly. "Renee—"

"Leave me alone!" Renee cried, raising her hand.

Cortez watched her a moment longer before he turned to head out of the room.

Chapter 16

Justin McNeil propped one hand alongside his handsome face. He frowned, listening to one of his top producers on the other end of the phone. "Julia, when are you coming back to work?" he asked for the third time.

Sighing, Julia closed her eyes against the sun reflecting brightly off the pool. "I'm still on vacation, Justin," she reminded him in a singsong tone.

"I thought that was over."

"I've never taken a vacation. You know how much time I have saved up. Besides, just because I'm home doesn't mean I can't relax."

Justin didn't like the hollow tone in Julia's usually boisterous voice. He figured she must be going through something intense, so he didn't push. "Listen...take your time, all right? Call me anytime if you need anything, you hear?"

Julia smiled. "Thanks, Justin. I will."

"So, um…what's the deal with Cortez Wallace? The guys are gonna ask, you know."

Julia pressed her lips together and willed her voice to come out strong. "I already told Ken that they shouldn't keep their hopes up about wooing him out here. I'm pretty sure that it's a closed subject now."

Justin nodded. "I'll let 'em know."

Clearing her throat, Julia hissed a silent curse at the pressure she felt behind her eyes. "Justin, I need to go, okay?"

"All right, honey, I'll talk to you soon."

"Okay. Bye."

Julia sat the black cordless phone on the glass table and leaned back against the lounge chair. She knew it would be better to stay busy, but she'd felt so beaten up after the trip. Now she just wanted to hide out and lick her wounds.

"And what better place to do that than right here at my pool," she said out loud, glancing down at the skimpy bikini she wore. The two-piece creation had practically been her only attire since she returned home.

Her thoughts were interrupted a few moments later when she heard the doorbell ring. For a while she debated on whether or not to answer. Unfortunately, the ringing became so insistent that she decided to at least see who it was. Pushing herself off the cushiony chaise, she walked barefoot through her airy L.A. home. Pulling off her sunglasses, she stood on her toes and looked through the peephole. Her breath caught in her throat and she backed away from the door as though she had been burned.

After a moment, she pulled the door open. She slowly lifted her head to meet Cortez Wallace's handsome caramel face.

"Julia." The sexy baritone greeting held just the slightest trace of helplessness.

Julia's heart pounded in her ears, almost deafening her. She had never been more shocked to see anyone in her life.

Cortez was just as shocked, as his eyes inadvertently trailed the luscious dark length of Julia's body. The sky blue bikini she wore left little to the imagination, making it almost impossible to look away. "May I come inside?" he managed to ask.

Julia's eyes fluttered shut at the soft, unintentionally suggestive request. Her legs actually weakened beneath her, causing her to sway a little.

"Juli," Cortez whispered, catching her in his strong embrace.

She inhaled the clean, enticing scent of his cologne and wanted to melt against the hard wall of his chest. Taking control of her emotions, she braced herself and pushed away. "What do you want? What are you doing out here?"

"I wanted to apologize," he explained, pushing his hands deep into the pockets of his dark denim jeans.

Julia cast a glance over her shoulder. "My phone's working."

Cortez was ever so humble as he bowed his head. "This was something I needed to do in person."

Julia gave a quick nod. "Well, you did it. Now you can leave." She began to push the door closed.

Cortez placed one hand around the edge of the door, stopping her. "I know you didn't sleep with Correll."

"How?" Julia asked, her dark eyes snapping to his face.

Cortez took a step closer. "He told me."

Julia's lips parted in surprise. She stepped aside and held the door open for him.

"I'm sorry," he said.

Julia shut her eyes, not wanting to see the hurt in Cortez's face, "Why don't you tell me about Correll?"

Cortez walked around the living room, retelling the story in explicit detail. He left nothing out. Meanwhile, Julia simply stood there like a statue. She clenched her fists so tightly that her long nails left deep impressions in her palms.

"Julia? Are you listening to me?"

Julia dropped to the sofa, tracing the elaborate patterns in the cushions with her teary eyes.

"I feel like hell over this. I should've listened to you," he admitted, kneeling beside her.

Julia's eyes rose from the sofa to Cortez's face. In the next instant, she reared back and slapped him hard.

"You're damn right you should've listened to me!" Julia bellowed, jumping to her feet. "You jackass! I tried to explain this to you. Twice! Each time you refused to hear anything I had to say. Your precious brother and fiancée cooked up this crap and you fell for it! I don't know if I'm angrier at you for being such an idiot or myself for being stupid enough to chase after your foolish ass!"

"Julia—"

"Get out!" She pounded her fist once against the front of his Piston's T-shirt.

Cortez knew nothing would be settled that day, but he couldn't leave without telling her. "She wasn't my fiancée."

"What?" She whirled around to face him.

Cortez focused on the impression made by his thumb when he drove it into his palm. "Renee wasn't my fiancée. She never was."

"I knew it," Julia breathed. Losing her strength to remain on her feet, she returned to the sofa. "Why?"

Her lost tone of voice was like a barb through his side. He ached to go to her but didn't dare move any closer than he already was. "When you came to Detroit, all I wanted was for you to go." He shrugged, slowly bringing his gaze back to her face. "Clearly I would've done anything to make that happen."

"So the story really was a lie?"

"Renee let it get out of hand intentionally and I went along with it. We *were* seen around town together a lot." Cortez massaged the ache as it began to take root in his chest. "They were usually live appearances, but many times it was a meal out somewhere to discuss a story. I swear it was always about business, Juli."

Julia, however, was on the verge of shock. "I knew it was a lie, but I still can't believe you'd do all this just to get me to leave you alone." She looked up at him finally with a pair of teary eyes. "Did you hate me that much, Cork?"

Cortez closed his eyes. The pain in his side was twisting with a vengeance.

"What am I supposed to do with this? With knowing all this?" She was staring at her hands clenched in her lap.

"You said you suspected it all along?"

"I hoped." She uttered a half-hearted laugh. "I figured hearing you say it would—"

He made a move toward her. "I can't make this up to you, Julia," he said when she flinched from his touch. "But I can't go, either."

She laughed long and fully. "Why not? It's what you wanted, right?"

"It's not what I wanted. Only...what I felt I had to do."

"So I should take that to mean you did this because of your condescending family." She watched him as though he were a stranger. "All those years, I thought you were better than them, above their pettiness."

"Juli—"

"Don't! You're as sick and as tiny-minded as they are!" Leaning on her anger, she pushed off the sofa and bolted across the room to glare past the windows.

"I love you, Julia. I swear I never stopped."

Tears spurted out of Julia's eyes and rolled down her cheeks as she turned her face away from Cortez. She wanted to believe him and give in. Unfortunately, fear and hurt prevented her from doing that.

Cortez walked up behind Julia, pulling her back against his solid, warm body. "Juli, now it's my turn to beg for a chance," he whispered into her ear, caressing the soft lobe with his lips.

Julia felt her body respond instantly. Her entire body vibrated lightly as Cortez cupped her breasts in his hands. She fought the urge to move against him. But when his fingers brushed the moistening center of her bikini bottom, Julia knew she was about to give in. She stiffened in his arms and pushed his hands away from her body.

"Go, Cortez." Her voice was breathless from arousal.

Nodding, he stroked the light beard covering his face and stepped away from her. He decided to give her space, for a while. He left his hotel name and number on the back of his card before leaving.

Chapter 17

Julia frowned when she saw the blaring, red numbers on her bedside clock. She couldn't believe she was awake at 8:30 in the morning, when lately she had been rising around noon. Still, she pulled herself from the inviting, king-size four-poster bed. Her sleep had been interrupted several times that night by unnerving dreams. She just couldn't get Cortez out of her mind. All night she dreamed of them making love. It seemed so real that she awoke many times to find herself moist from the vivid images. She woke up cursing herself for still thinking about him between her legs after all she'd gone through because of him.

Shaking away her heated thoughts, Julia washed her face and brushed her teeth. Then she headed downstairs to the kitchen. Her objective was to fix breakfast, but the thought of Cortez's surprise visit kept coming to mind. As she'd suspected, the engagement was a sham. Her thoughts were muddled yesterday, but now she could lock in on what she couldn't say to him then. Hearing him confess it—he'd carried on the lie while she'd spent her nights guilt-ridden and calling herself every name in the book for interfering with his relationship with Renee. Then there was the topper: her supposed romp with Correll. Cortez was only there now because he'd discovered that that, too, was a lie, she thought.

In spite of it all, Julia had to smile while adding peppers and onions to her omelet mixture. If only Cortez had waited on his brother to intervene, he'd have gotten rid of her without having to go to all the other trouble.

Her amusement faded then and she leaned against the counter wearily. Therein lay the answer to all her questions about what to do with Cortez Wallace's change of heart. Had she slept with his brother, willingly or not, he'd have never forgiven her the way he was asking her to do with regards to his own actions. Simply put: the man she loved would never be able to trust her word.

Julia continued to think about this as she cooked breakfast. She was removing the cheese hash browns from the stove when the doorbell rang. Frowning, she tightened the belt around her short, silk mauve robe and left the kitchen.

When she peeked out and saw Cortez on the porch, her eyes narrowed in suspicion. Sighing, she pressed her head against the door. *I don't need this. If he keeps coming here, I'll give in.*

Her silent words were interrupted when the doorbell rang again. Bracing herself, she pulled the door open.

"Good morning." Cortez greeted her with, a devilish grin brightening his very attractive face.

"What now?"

Cortez's heavenly brown eyes narrowed for an instant. "Grouchy in the morning, aren't you?"

Julia propped her hand on her hip as her eyebrows rose. "Well, you wouldn't know how I am in the morning, would you?"

Cortez propped his tall, lean frame against the door and towered over her. "Not lately. But that's something I hope to change," he softly assured her.

Julia's heart flew to her throat and she stepped back. "What do you want, Cortez?"

His expression turned helpless. "You know what I want."

Julia turned away and Cortez took that as his cue to enter the house.

"Are you cooking?"

Julia slammed her door shut. "Yeah, breakfast. For *myself*."

"Would you like some company?"

Julia didn't respond, though the look in her black eyes screamed no, She watched him walk through her home as though he owned it. "My kitchen isn't upstairs," she told him when he made a move in that direction.

He waited for her to lead the way. When she walked past him he pushed his hands into the pockets of the black nylon jogging pants he wore and trained his gaze on her slender form. The material of her robe wasn't skin-tight, but it did offer an arousing outline of her bottom. A grin cast a sinister element across his face as he dismissed what ran through his mind. Their sex life had never been an issue and would never be until other, *real* issues were settled. Once they were in the kitchen, though, the delicious scents caught his attention again and he commented favorably.

"Listen, Cortez, I don't know what the hell you expect

from me now, but you can forget it." Julia said, ignoring his sunny disposition. "So you can just save all this new-found interest."

Cortez sighed and dropped his head. "I've always been interested in you," he said, raising his warm, chocolate smile to her face. "I admit it. I was fooling myself. I couldn't face the fact that I missed you, and when you came back to town I was so angry because you being there was making it impossible for me to deny that."

Julia turned back to the stove and began to melt extra cheese for her omelet. "And you just had to deny it because *I* was the one who left, right?"

Cortez shrugged his wide shoulders beneath the stylish, lightweight gray sweatshirt he wore. "Because you were right. You were right all along."

Julia threw down her spoon and pinned Cortez with an accusing glare. "You know what? Save it. I'm done. Finally, I'm done. This. Us. It's done. I can't do this to myself anymore."

Cortez leaned against the counter and looked down at her. "I can't walk away Juli, so please don't tell me to."

Julia watched him through her tears. "Then maybe you'll understand what it's been like for me."

When she bolted, preparing to leave the kitchen, his reflexes kicked in. He caught her arm, keeping it behind her back. She gasped, giving him the opportunity to thrust his mouth upon hers.

Her legs turned to liquid and she moaned beneath the deep, sensuous caress. If possible, the kiss intensified and Julia arched herself into Cortez's lean, muscular frame.

"Wait, Cortez…" Julia weakly resisted, when he broke the kiss to let his lips trail her neck. "Wait." She began to struggle against him.

Cortez let go of Julia's arm and slid both of his around

her waist. It seemed surprisingly effortless, considering Julia's determination to get away from him. A pained smile pulled at his mouth in response to her fighting to push him off. Ignoring that, he buried his face into the cleft of her breasts and inhaled her scent.

At that moment, Julia wanted Cortez more than she ever did. She just couldn't allow herself to give in, but fighting didn't seem to be working. It was like pitting wind against a tree, so she used a different tactic.

"Cortez, please stop this. I can't fight you, but I can't do this."

She was right. Damn it all. She was right. He needed to leave before he forgot that. Releasing her slowly, he nuzzled her temple and did as she'd asked.

Julia felt the heat of his body leave hers. She closed her eyes and refused to cry.

Chapter 18

Julia never looked forward to Mondays. Still, she felt surprisingly optimistic when she stepped into the corridor of her office that morning. She decided to view that Monday as a beginning in much the same way she'd decided to look at her whole life—one big, new beginning. With any hope, Cortez was realizing this wouldn't be the easy win he'd expected and go home. She'd successfully pushed to the back of her mind the voice that kept reminding her that she loved him and needed to stop denying it.

The hall was gloriously void of bodies and gave Julia another cause for celebration. No need to stop and make morning conversation about who did what and where for the weekend. She floated into her office, the flaring hem of her figure-flattering mushroom silk dress accentuating her legs. She slung her tote to the settee near her desk and then settled in to begin checking her e-mails and phone messages. The thought of coffee crossed her mind and Julia figured it'd be best to get it before the rest of the office began filing in. She was still standing behind the desk when the office door opened and Lexi poked her head inside.

"Hey, Ken wanted you in his office ten minutes ago."

"What for?" Julia made no move to hasten her steps.

Lexi's shrug caused her ponytail to swing merrily. "No idea, but he's in there with all the guys, including Mr. Wallace."

Refusing to react to that bit of info, Julia began to make her way to the front of the office. She ignored the curiosity in her assistant's eyes and held her head high as she made her way to Kenrick Owen's office suite. She was fighting to hold onto her sunny Monday outlook, but a tiny niggling was starting to eat away at the edges of that outlook. Looking on the *sunny* side, Julia decided it was better to get the crap out of the way early. That way she could look forward to a full day of great things, right?

When she got to Ken's office, knocked once and stepped inside, she had confirmation that the crap would be falling hard and heavy at length that day. Ken was laughing.

"Julia! We were just about to take a drive to your place and deliver the news!"

"What news?" Her dark eyes were fixed on Cortez standing across the room.

Bennett Daniels walked over to bring Julia into the office. He eased her into one of the deep armchairs before the stunning pine desk and patted her back in a subtly reassuring manner.

"Our man Cortez has accepted our job offer," Ken announced.

Julia was grateful for the chair. She only blinked, desperate to stop the urge to bristle at the look in his smoky stare. Those warm brown orbs held a glint that confirmed he knew she was livid.

The guys were thrilled, of course. Kenrick was going on about meetings and deciding on debut show tapings and the like. Julia couldn't take it, and, feeling sick amidst all the chatter, she rushed out moments later with her hand clamped over her mouth.

Cortez wasn't far behind.

Julia commended herself on fending off the nausea until she made it home. She didn't bother closing the front door behind her but raced to the closest bathroom and cursed herself viciously when the sickness never materialized. She stumbled from the bath, making a half-hearted attempt at closing her door and frowning when the lock didn't catch. She stiffened when she discovered why.

"Get out." She rolled her eyes and strolled from the foyer on surprisingly strong legs. "Go brainstorm ideas for your new show."

Cortez shut the front door and followed the path she took to the kitchen. There he leaned on one side of the arched doorway and watched her guzzle two glasses of tap water. His gaze was hooded as he studied her intently. They needed to talk, *really* talk, but he'd finally accepted that for him that would be impossible. He couldn't think straight until he had her.

Julia bristled the instant she felt his hands cupping her waist. Moments later he turned her around. Lifting her without effort, he placed her on the countertop. He made quick work of the button-down top of the curve-hugging dress she'd chosen for the day. Once the tiny row of pearl buttons was undone, he brought his persuasive lips to the valley between her breasts. Strong teeth tugged at the front of Julia's dress, as it was pulled away to reveal her breasts.

Cortez leaned back and traced the round, flawless dark globes with his glorious, talented tongue. He licked his lips before settling them to the tip of one mound. Closing his eyes, he savored the sweet, unfamiliar taste of her skin.

Julia's weak cry filled the kitchen when she felt his passionate tugging at her nipples. She arched her back, pushing more of herself into Cortez's hot mouth.

Cortez moaned when he felt the slight movement. Pushing the dress fully away from her shoulders, his fingers caressed her bare skin and pulled her even closer.

Shivers of delight danced along Julia's spine and she gasped. Throwing her head back, she threw her doubts and caution and questions aside. She was sick of fighting and ready to take what she wanted.

Cortez lowered his hands to Julia's thighs and squeezed their luscious length. He pushed against her dress hem and stockings until they became too much of a hindrance and were discarded. Julia squirmed against the countertop as Cortez took turns suckling the firm tips of her breasts. He mimicked the action of soothing her nipples with his tongue by caressing her through the drenched middle of her panties with both of his thumbs. He soon pulled the wispy lace away. His fingers sank into her well and he groaned into Julia's neck.

When Cortez pulled her off the counter, Julia was helpless to do anything but cling to him. She locked her long legs around his back, aching to feel as much of his impressive erection as possible.

"Where?"

"Upstairs," Julia moaned, shivering from the air touching her nude body and the deep timbre of his voice.

Cortez chuckled and pressed a quick kiss to her cheek. "Where upstairs?"

"Last door on the left," she softly instructed, as her head dropped to his shoulder.

Julia couldn't have cared less where Cortez set her down as long as he made love to her. He took the plush, carpeted stairs two at a time, quickly approaching the bedroom. He didn't bother with the lamp, using the sunlight streaming around the drawn tan drapes in the room to find his way.

Gently, he placed Julia in the center of the bed. For a moment, he watched her.

Then, in one smooth movement, he pulled off his charcoal suit coat and silver-gray shirt. Julia's slanted gaze widened at his chiseled muscular chest and abdomen.

Cortez braced himself on his steely forearms and began to place moist, baby-soft kisses on Julia's feet. His tongue traced the smooth line of her calf, stopping to nibble at the soft skin behind her knee.

Julia gasped and arched her body off the bed. "Cortez!"

"Mmm?" He absently replied, kissing her inner thigh. "What?" he asked teasingly, this time his breath beating against her sex.

"Promise not to stop," Julia moaned, unashamed.

"I hadn't planned to," he assured her, just before his tongue plunged deep inside her. He was like a man starved for the taste of her as he drank from the center of her body.

When the pleasure became unbearable, Julia tried to close her legs. Cortez wouldn't allow it. He pressed his large hands across her thighs to hold them apart. After a while he moved on, trailing the kisses farther up her body and stopping at her belly button.

Julia wasn't used to playing such a passive role in bed, but with Cortez it felt so good. Every stroke of his tongue and hands made her breathless with want.

His hands on her thighs made it impossible to move, and the pleasure consumed her more powerfully as a result. He intermingled the ragged thrusts of his tongue inside her body with wet kisses slathered across her inner thighs. Julia cried out shamelessly, rolling her head to and fro as her breath staggered. She brought her hands to her chest and squeezed her breasts wantonly. Her helpless cries ended in a pleasure-filled shriek when Cortez bit softly on one of the silken folds guarding her femininity.

Thoroughly enraptured, Julia had no choice but to lie there and take whatever Cortez chose to give her. It was a choice she was happy to accept. That acceptance, however, beckoned her climax all the more quickly and powerfully. Satisfied by her reaction, Cortez pulled back to watch her in the throes of the ecstasy he'd caused. He removed what remained of his clothing and returned to the bed. where he shuddered in pleasure at the feel of her body naked and trembling next to his.

Once protection was in place, his lips fastened onto the pouting tips of her breasts, and he pushed one knee between her legs. Again, he gripped her thighs and held them apart. A ragged groan was torn from his chest as he slowly thrust himself inside.

Julia pulled her lower lip between her teeth and savored

the feel of her tight heat gripping the sensuous length of his sex. Very slowly she began to move against him and gasped at the sensation.

"Don't move," Cortez ordered, squeezing her hips while hiding his face in her neck. Apparently he was savoring the delicious feel of her femininity surrounding him, as well.

Julia obeyed the soft command and waited for Cortez to take the lead. When he did, she instantly joined in on the pleasurable task.

Soft cries and deep moans filled the room as their lovemaking became more forceful. Julia couldn't believe it was happening after all this time. Cortez knew nothing would ever compare.

Julia left for work before Cortez woke the next morning. She wouldn't admit that cowardice had anything to do with her eagerness to get a jump on the day. At the office, she plunged into work, which included a few preliminary ideas Kenrick had left regarding the new show with Cortez. She was already deep into jotting notes for an upcoming meeting of the first taping when Lexi stuck her head past the office door.

Julia waved her inside. A suspicious frown crept across her face at the sight of Lexie's huge grin. When Cortez followed the woman inside the office, Julia's suspicion was confirmed.

Lexi waved her hand toward one of the chairs facing the desk. "Can I get you anything? Coffee, tea, danish, juice?"

Cortez favored Lexi with a gorgeous grin and shook his head. "No, I appreciate it, but I'm fine."

Lexi's wide, blue eyes narrowed as she took stock of the tall man before her. "Yes, you are," she breathed, and then shook her head, realizing she had spoken aloud. "I mean, um, okay. If you'll excuse me I'll just get going."

Julia grimaced, watching as her usually reserved assistant tripped all over Cortez. "Thanks, Lexi," she called to her as she walked back out through the doorway.

Julia stood and smoothed her hands over her form-fitting mocha dress. Cortez let his eyes rake the length of her body appreciatively. When Julia sat perched on the edge of her desk, he reached out to stroke her bare thigh.

"You were dead to the world when I left. You obviously had a very good time yesterday."

Cortez grinned, remembering their day together. "I had a very good time," he assured her. "I dare you to deny it was one of your best," he said, his cocky demeanor rising to the surface.

Not wanting to risk Cortez's ego becoming more inflated, Julia decided not to respond. Instead, she eased off the desk and walked around him. "You weren't seeing the real me yesterday."

Amused, Cortez tilted his head back to stare at her. "The real you?"

"Mmm-hmm," Julia confirmed, stooping next to his chair. "If submission is what you want in a lover, then you've got the wrong woman."

"Can you clarify that?" Cortez asked as he stared down at her. His laughter was close to the surface.

"Well, you know how aggressive I can be," she said, gazing at him naughtily. "I assure you it doesn't end at the workplace."

Cortez nodded. "Aggression isn't bad, if kept in its place," he said, enjoying their wordplay.

"In its place?" Julia finished for him, now standing

over the chair. "You know, Cortez, you may want to think twice about accepting this show. Aggression kept out of its place makes many men uneasy."

"Do you think I'm one of those men?"

"I guess we'll see," Julia retorted, crossing her arms over her chest.

Cortez remained cool, still enjoying their banter. "I only like control in the bedroom," he said, on the brink of laughter when her lips parted.

"I like control, too," Julia assured him. "Complete control."

"Then we have something in common," Cortez replied, picking up her silent challenge.

Julia threw her hands in the air and laughed. "I think that's where we have our problem."

"It doesn't have to be a problem."

Julia's brows rose and she simply planted herself astride his lap. Cortez's massive hands caressed the toned, luscious length of her thighs and she was instantly aroused.

"Does that mean you're planning to give in?" she asked. "Accept that perhaps this isn't the best idea."

In reply, one of his hands cupped the back of her neck and pulled her down to meet his kiss.

Julia moaned weakly when Cortez thrust his tongue deep into her mouth. Her insides turned to mush and she thrust herself against him, grinding her hips erotically.

They both cursed when a knock sounded at the door. With effort, Julia pulled herself off Cortez's lap and walked across the office.

Lexi stood outside the door with two envelopes in her hand. "Kenrick sent me here with card keys to the suite for the announcement party at the Pierre. One is for Mr. Wallace, and he's free to bring a guest, if he wants."

"Thanks, Lexi," Julia said, taking the small, white

cards. Then she closed the door on the woman's prying eyes. She reluctantly gave Cortez the envelope before tossing hers to the desk. Massaging her temples, she struggled with the right way to say what needed to be said and then decided to just come right out with it. "I don't see this working, Cork. This show, us working together with all this," she waved her hands back and forth between the two of them.

Cortez grinned and slid his thumb across the sleek line of his brow. "Juli, when have we *not* had all this between us?"

"We've never slept *and* worked together before."

Tensing then, Cortez let the muscle dance viciously along his jaw before he stood. "So easy for you to forget eight years ago, isn't it?"

She stiffened at the accusation. "This is different. I've got a reputation to think about."

"Are you saying I'm not good for it?"

Julia gave a nervous tug at a flaring sleeve of her mocha dress. "I'm *saying* that it's one I've worked hard to build. Unlike the one I was *given* in Detroit, this is one I'm damn proud of." Her expression changed and she looked away. "In spite of my achievements here, there're a helluva lot of folks around here who believe I got where I am by sleeping around." She fixed Cortez with a challenging look. "Now what do you think our sleeping together is gonna do for that train of thought?"

"Since when do you care?" He asked, not quite believing the words that had come from her mouth.

"I care since—" Julia couldn't stop her voice from shaking with emotion "—since a trumped-up rep was what cost me the man I loved. Because one self-centered, snotty woman felt I came from too far across the tracks to be good enough for her son. That was eight years ago and that lie is still costing me him to this day."

"Juli…" Cortez bowed his head and massaged the bridge of his nose.

She stepped close, hands outstretched. "Just please think about this, okay? For me?"

The weariness in her eyes broke his heart. He simply nodded, leaned down to press a kiss to her forehead and left her to her thoughts.

Chapter 19

Julia popped a plump Bay scallop into her mouth and savored the taste. The buffet was a smorgasbord of delectable seafood, beautiful vegetables and sinful desserts.

After adding a few more scallops to the mound of treats on her plate, Julia moved on. Her dark eyes scanned the crowded suite at the Pierre for Cortez, but he was nowhere in sight.

Maybe you got through to him, she told herself, not really believing she'd be so lucky. Then there was the twinge of pain she felt over the reality of him leaving for good.

"Are you with us, girl?"

Julia blinked several times, focusing on two of her coworkers and friends. Marisa Delon and Collette Fredericks were watching her closely. "Sorry, what's up?" she asked the two women.

Collette glanced over her shoulder and then pinned Julia with a wicked stare. "Why don't you tell us about our newest asset, Cortez Wallace?"

"Cortez?"

"Honey, yes, Cortez. I didn't know you knew him."

Julia smoothed her hands throughout her hair and gave Marisa a serious look. "Yeah, we're old friends."

"That's all?" Collette shrieked in disbelief and tossed her bouncy black hair from her round, pretty face. "Girl, he is far too fine to be roaming the streets of L.A. alone."

"Please, Collette, Julia knows that all too well," Marisa decided.

Julia couldn't help but laugh. "Y'all are too much!"

"So come on. Tell me all about him," Collette whispered, taking a small step closer.

Julia shrugged her shoulders. "What do you want to know?"

"I can't say we haven't all been wondering if you and Julia are a little more than old friends, my man."

Cortez grinned, confirming Ken's assumption. "We have been for quite a while, but we're still not as close as I'd like us to be."

Ken nodded, rubbing the side of his face. "She's the best person on our team."

"That's what I hear. She's made a real name for herself," Cortez remarked, realizing what Justin was getting at.

"She's earned it," Justin said, tossing back the rest of his cognac.

"I know she has."

"Cortez, man, I hope you don't take offense here, but I've got to ask if there's any major drama between you two."

Cortez was struck by a sudden bout of laughter.

Kenrick replied in turn. "I guess that's my answer, then."

Swallowing a bit more of the drink he'd been nursing, Cortez considered his next statement. "I love her to obsession," he confessed, as his eyes wandered over to Julia, where she stood talking with coworkers. "I've also hurt her more times than I can count. And now, when I most need her to, I don't think she'll ever trust me again."

Ken's expression grew serious. Heavy brows rose. "So how's this gonna affect the two of you working so closely together?" He glanced over at Julia then, too. "You guys are gonna butt heads a lot. How much of that'll be about the show and how much will be about unfinished personal business?"

"You know, Ken—" Cortez didn't mind letting his unease show and tapped back what was left of his drink "—I'm real glad you brought that up."

The candlelit patio looked like something straight off of a movie set. Julia always hid out there whenever Justin's parties began to grate on her nerves. The peaceful atmosphere always helped her forget whatever frustrated her.

Unfortunately, the purely romantic aura of the patio did nothing for her that night. If anything, it made her think about Cortez. God, if only she could take him at his word...

Shaking her head, Julia pulled an invisible speck of lint from her shimmery, gold halter gown and decided to head back to the party. When she turned, he was standing there in the arched doorway.

Without a word, Cortez walked across the patio until

he stood before her. One large hand cupped her cheek, his thumb caressing her flawless molasses-toned skin.

Julia's eyes closed at his feather-soft touch and she pressed her face against it. Cortez frowned slightly as he studied the weary, drawn expression on her oval face. Instead of questioning it, he pulled her closer.

Melting against his warm, chiseled form, Julia sighed her content. The soft music drifting out onto the patio, combined with the relaxing outdoors, was intoxicating.

"Julia! Girl, we've been lookin' everywhere for you!"

Cortez and Julia jumped apart at the sound of the two male voices. Julia gave Matthew Mayes and Jerry Orned tiny smiles, while Cortez just watched them.

"Hey, guys. What's up?"

Matthew and Jerry were approaching Cortez with extended hands. "We've been trying to get an introduction to this guy all night," Jerry said.

A smile finally appeared on Cortez's face as he shook hands with the two men. "Cortez Wallace."

"Cortez, this is Matthew Mayes and Jerry Orned. They're coanchors on our early-morning news show," Julia was saying.

"Good to meet a fellow anchor," Matthew said.

"Same here." Cortez replied, his words tinged with laughter.

"We only wanted to congratulate you on the show," Jerry Orned explained.

"You're a lucky man to be working with our Julia," Matthew tacked on.

"Thanks. That much I know." Cortez didn't mask anything when he looked at her.

Julia was relieved that Matthew and Jerry hadn't noticed.

"You've already got a slew of envious coworkers in your midst, kid," Jerry teased.

Julia laughed right along, but the gesture wasn't nearly as full and rich as that of her male cohorts.

Cortez was chuckling as loudly as anyone. "Sorry to hear that, but I can't say working with her is gonna be a hardship."

"Would you guys excuse me?" The request was soft, demure and effectively masked her agitation. Without a word to anyone, Julia left the party.

Julia didn't rest until she had made it back home. By that time, it was raining buckets. The air was very cool and she shivered as the heavy droplets of water beat against her bare skin. Leaving her car parked sideways in the driveway, she ran inside the house.

Stripping off her drenched dress, Julia tiptoed out of the foyer. She hurried across the thick living-room carpet and lit the logs already in the fireplace. Waiting for the heat to rise, she stood there rubbing her bare arms. There was a fluffy, gray blanket on one of the armchairs and she wrapped it around her nude body.

As soon as the logs began to crackle beneath the orange flames, Julia's thoughts turned to Cortez. He'd always be around to remind her of the unwarranted talk that had consistently followed her in Detroit. He was only there now because he'd confirmed she was innocent of an indiscretion with his brother and not because he believed her when she'd told him so. The reality of it was wreaking havoc on her heart, her head and her body.

The bell rang and silently Julia cursed the sound. Cortez, she predicted. Refusing to answer the door would only add increased pettiness to the situation. Grumbling, she stalked through the living room and chose to meet the situation head-on. By the time she pulled open the door, she was praying for the will to at least make eye contact. Cortez stood there drenched, but sexy as ever.

"I don't feel like talking," she managed.

He shook his head. "Good. Neither do I."

Cortez took hold and pulled her to him. His wide, sensuous mouth pressed into hers in a hard, possessive kiss that forced a moan just past her lips. She instantly melted beneath the slow, rhythmic thrusts of his tongue as her fingers stroked the crisp whiskers of his beard.

When he broke the kiss, Julia's enchanting gaze searched Cortez's intense brown eyes. As she stood there, staring into his face, her legs suddenly went weak beneath her. She slid right out of Cortez's embrace to the furry rug before the fireplace.

Cortez opened the blanket Julia had wrapped around her body. His gorgeous cocoa stare caressed every inch of her dark form before he permitted himself to touch her. His strong fingers circled her full breasts, while his lips enclosed their firm peaks one at a time.

Julia stroked the back of Cortez's neck as she enjoyed the slow, arousing strokes of his tongue against her nipples. As his thumb brushed the other hard peak, she ground her hips against his. The impressive bulge between his legs caused her to gasp.

The flames were still roaring in the huge, stone fireplace as the rainstorm continued outside. Julia and Cortez felt as though they were locked away in their own sensual world, and they enjoyed the pleasures of making love all night.

Chapter 20

Heavy raindrops still beat against the window the next morning. Julia snuggled deeper beneath the thick lime green comforter and sighed. She turned and stared at the empty space next to her. Cortez was gone, but in his place there was a small note. Julia pressed the folded paper to her face and smiled. The message was brief, but very sweet. He promised to see her later that evening.

The phone on the shiny maple nightstand began to ring. Julia snatched the receiver up, hoping to hear Cortez's voice.

"Yes?"

"Hey, Jukee, what's up?"

"Monique! Honey, what's goin' on?" Julia greeted her sister, equally pleased to hear her voice.

"Girl, Mama just told me that Cortez was in California with you. I can't believe it! Did he call off the wedding or somethin'?"

Julia sat up in bed. "There never was one. It was all a lie—like I said."

"How..." Monique sighed. "Did *he* say—"

"*He* said, Mo," Julia shrugged. "It's a very long story." She smothered a yawn.

"Mmm...I hear ya," Monique agreed. "Well, listen, I didn't call to talk about that anyway. You do remember that Dad's birthday is in a few weeks?"

Julia slapped her palm against her forehead. "Damn. Thanks for reminding me, Mo. Have you started any planning yet?"

"We're almost set. You just make sure you get your butt back here."

"Don't worry. I wouldn't miss Daddy's party for the world."

"Good...and Julia, sweetie, be careful with Cortez, all right? I know how much you've wanted this, but keep your eyes open, okay?"

Julia inhaled deeply. "I plan to do exactly that. Thanks, Mo."

Later that day, Julia was in her usual spot behind the desk in her office, toiling away. She brought a quick end to her call with the editing department when her office door opened and Ken stepped in along with Cortez.

"Did I forget a meeting?" she asked, noting their closed expressions.

Ken shook his head. "No, Julia. We've, um, decided to pull you from the coproducer chair on Cortez's show."

"Wha—" Julia couldn't complete the word and sat openmouthed, her eyes darting back and forth between the two men.

"Everything is still a go for your own show. Nothing's changed regarding that." Ken cleared his throat while he clenched his hands nervously. "Even better—now you've got the go-ahead, the resources *and* the time to move forward full steam with it. I'll, uh—" he shot a quick glance toward Cortez "—I'll just leave you two to…talk." He gave Cortez a quick shoulder pat and hustled out of the room.

Still speechless, Julia looked to Cortez for clarification.

"I want to be where you are," he told her simply, his easy stride bringing him closer to the desk. "You won't be comfortable working with me on the show, and I'll do what it takes to prove I don't intend to lose you. I've got every intention of making this work."

Julia tugged on the ends of the lightweight pine scarf she wore. "I don't know what to say," she admitted, which was more than a little true. Her show was a go, which was what she'd wanted all along, and it was because of Cortez. She wasn't altogether sure *how* to feel about that.

Lips curved into a knowing smile as he leaned across the desk. "Don't say a thing," he planted a kiss to her temple. "Just go home and pack."

She regained her balance after several sweet seconds. "Pack?"

"How did you know I had a weakness for Big Bear?" Julia asked, her dark gaze wide as black moons while taking in the exquisite wintry scene before her.

Cortez maneuvered the SUV through the snowy terrain with the skill of a seasoned professional. "Lexi told me when I asked about your favorite things to do to unwind." The sexy curve of his mouth tilted into a smirk. "Sad thing was, she said you never take off the time to come here."

Julia shrugged and took a refreshing breath. "My life's been my work."

"Let's see if we can change that."

With reluctance, Julia tugged her eyes away from the mountain scene beyond the passenger window. "Cortez, what are you doing?"

He didn't answer. She hadn't expected him to be ready with a reply and urged herself to just enjoy this for what it was: an impromptu getaway.

She scarcely noticed when he parked the truck at an angle before a tiny cottage. The resort boasted a mountain lodge with two four-star restaurants, a twenty-four-hour café and bar. Guests resided in the rugged yet plush cottages dotting the grand expanse of the property.

Cortez left the truck and then walked around to open Julia's door. When she moved to jump out, he stopped her.

"What I'm doing is trying to get back in here." He brushed the back of his hand against her heart.

In spite of the frigid temperatures, Julia felt like melting. The words stoked her love and desire for him all at once. Linking her arms around his neck, she took his mouth in a throaty kiss that sizzled as a helpless moan vibrated in the back of his throat.

Keeping her against him and never breaking the kiss, Cortez carried Julia from the SUV. He kicked the passenger door shut with the tip of his boot and headed for the cabin door. Julia shivered when a wave of heat replaced the chill of the air. Weakly, her eyes fluttered as she tried to observe her surroundings. Cortez's kiss, however, removed any desire to do anything other than continue kissing him.

He didn't stop, but continued walking until he stood in the middle of the bedroom. Effortlessly, he continued to carry Julia, now cradling her full backside in his palms. Massaging the globes encased beneath her jeans, he deepened the kiss while pressing her more firmly into the stiffness straining the zipper of his jeans.

Julia raked her nails across his rough jaw. She tried to breathe amidst the onslaught of the kiss and didn't care that she couldn't. Her entire body was on fire for him, yet she tried to stifle her urges against being too aggressive. Cortez must've sensed that, for his touch was blatantly teasing. He sat on the bed, having her straddle him there and continuing the enticing duel between their tongues.

Weakly, Julia ground herself against him. She could have become orgasmic simply from the delicious friction of his shaft nudging her center.

"Cortez, please," she moaned, when he halted her grinding by lifting her a tad off his lap.

"What do you want?" He hid his gorgeous face in her neck and intentionally goaded her.

Losing the war with herself, Julia released a frustrated sound and pushed him to his back. A moment later she was out of her ski jacket along with the matching sweater and the bra beneath it.

"That's it," Cortez muttered, allowing his hands free rein over her dark skin.

Julia bit her lip while he cupped her breasts and flicked his thumbs across her nipples. She bowed her head and lavished his face and neck with sweet kisses as she sought the bulge pushing against his jeans.

Cortez cupped her hips, lifting her easily until her breasts were neatly perked before his mouth. Julia wilted when he drew a nipple past his perfect teeth. The suckling sounds that resulted filled them both with increased sensation. Giving into his needs of aggression, Cortez flipped her beneath him and made quick work of unfastening her jeans. Julia wedged her feet from the cozy coral-colored ski boots that matched the sweater

she'd worn. When she was clothed in only the flimsiest
of panties, he began to pleasure her. Draping a lengthy
leg across his shoulder, he nudged his nose against the
moistening middle of the undergarment.

"Cortez..." She gasped, eager to feel him without his
clothing. "Please."

To silence her, he thrust his tongue deep into her mouth,
loving the helpless sound that followed. He skirted his
fingers along her trembling body and felt her shudder
when they glided ever so smoothly inside of her.

Once more Julia felt powerless to do more than
greedily absorb the delight he invoked. She rode three of
his fingers in wild abandon, softly ordering him not to
stop and to do what he was doing a little faster. When he
hinted at withdrawing, she clamped a hand on his wrist
and prevented him.

Cortez made do with his free hand, tugging his heavy
sweater and undershirt over his head. Julia released her
grip on his wrist to drag her nails across the flawless
expanse of his broad chest and shoulders. She scarcely
noticed him undoing his jeans and tugging them away
along with his boots and underwear. Her fingers explored
and massaged the soft hair that curved adorably over his
head, and she reveled in the feel of his bare chest against
hers.

He'd taken care of protection and held her thighs apart
to receive his body. Julia's nails dug into his skin and
created faint half-moon impressions where she gripped
him. Wavering moans rumbled from her throat as he
entered her, one beautifully stiff inch at a time.

He was still for a while once he was buried to the hilt.
Julia, however, moved desperately, and he could barely
hold out against the pleasure of it. Still, he wanted to relish
the feel of her, the feel of himself inside of her.

"I love you. I love you, Cortez...."

The sound of her voice next to his ear stripped his restraint. As though another switch had been turned on inside him, he captured her thighs in a vise grip and took her with fierce lunges that forced cries of pleasure from her throat.

Cortez rested his head on her chest, loving the sounds emerging every time he thrust deep into her wet sex. Soon, his own sounds of satisfaction were emerging and he was weakened completely. Julia took advantage, pushing him to his back again and taking him with a fierceness of her own. She braced herself when their fingers linked and circled her body erotically before rising up and down on the length that throbbed with life and power inside her.

Simultaneously, they came, exploding in a wave of love, need and want. Their linked fingers eventually weakened, and Julia slid down to lie across his chest. They remained there wilted and sated for a long while.

Cortez kissed her hair, inhaling its fragrance and dragging his fingers through the clipped dark locks. "Let's get dressed."

Julia would have laughed if she'd had the strength. "Now?" she managed.

"Mmm-hmm."

"*Right* now?"

"Right now," he confirmed.

"Why?" she whined. "What's the hurry?"

"Tell you what," he rose slightly, causing her to shriek and topple off, "We'll shower first."

"Why?" She whined again, tousling her hair as she frowned up at him. "Where are we going?"

He kissed the end of her nose. "Dinner."

"You okay?" Cortez asked, a smirk on his handsome face as he watched her eyes widen when she cleared the entryway of the cozy living room.

Julia simply nodded, taking in her lavish yet comfortable surroundings. The space was decorated with cream-and-gold furniture. Soft yellow light glowed from the candle-style lamps while flames blazed in the fireplace, casting their heat against the small, food-laden table next to it.

"When did you do this?" Julia whispered, walking farther into the room.

Cortez shrugged, "I had some time."

Julia whirled around to face him. "What are you up to? Really?" she asked.

Cortez's warm brown eyes narrowed as they roamed the length of her body. The sweater she wore outlined her heart-stopping curves. The mauve color flattered her flawless, dark complexion while the draping collar offered brief glimpses of bosom. Instead of giving Julia an answer to her question, he prepared two glasses of champagne.

Julia propped her hands on her hips, watching Cortez lift a glass of bubbly toward her. "What's the occasion?"

"Let's eat," Cortez said and offered his arm.

The silver serving dishes covering the table held succulent grilled chicken breasts in a light cream sauce, a zesty onion-and-broccoli dish, rice pilaf, salads and golden buttered rolls. It was all very delicious, but Julia could barely concentrate on it. Each time she raised her eyes across the table, she found Cortez watching her. His stare was so intense that it was unnerving.

"How was it?" Cortez asked later, once they had finished the coffee.

Julia wiped her mouth with a white linen cloth. "It was great. What's next?"

Pushing himself away from the table, Cortez walked over to help Julia out of her chair. "How about sitting in front of the fire?"

Already completely off balance by the events of the evening, Julia could only nod. Smoothing her hands over her comfy joggers, she let him lead her to the sofa next to the fire.

A loud gasp escaped Julia's lips when Cortez's mouth fell upon hers the moment they touched the sofa. She moaned in response to the slow, sensual thrusts of his tongue and arched herself close to his body, aching to feel his hands on her.

Cortez's large hands traveled the length of her thighs, and then he tore his lips from hers and settled them against her neck. The weight of his heavy, muscular form pressed Julia back into the cushiony sofa as his mouth trailed lower.

Julia threaded her fingers through his soft hair and enjoyed the caress of his lips. Just before he touched the generous swell of her breasts, he stopped.

"What's wrong?" Julia asked in a breathless tone, her midnight gaze wide.

"Will you marry me?" he asked, the look in his eyes as sincere as could be.

Julia blinked several times, knowing she'd heard him wrong. When she felt him push something cool and heavy onto her finger, she swallowed past the lump in her throat while staring at the glittering diamond. "Corky..."

Cortez pulled her up from the sofa and watched her. "Will you marry me?" he repeated.

Julia looked down at the fabulous ring and took a deep breath. "I—I can't."

"You what?" Cortez asked, the beginning of a frown starting to cloud his very handsome face.

"I can't marry you," Julia told him, her eyes still on the ring.

"You're saying no to me?" he asked, shocked. A deep crease had formed across his forehead.

Julia blinked the tears away from her eyes. "I'm sorry."

Cortez shook his head as if to clear it. "Are you serious?" he asked. "You said you loved me. Or was that just the moment talking?"

She winced. "You know that's not it."

"Then what?" Cortez whispered, his hands tightening around her arms. "Julia?"

She tilted her head to the side. "Cortez, I can't. I can't give you an answer now."

"Can you give me a reason?"

Julia stared into his eyes for a long time. She was about to lose herself in the sensual warmth of his gaze but refused to let that happen. She pushed herself away from him, unable to make herself tell him she believed he was only with her now because he had confirmation about Correll. "I just can't put myself through that again with you. Or your family. I just can't." She leaned on the most obvious reason.

"What the hell do they have to do with us?" Cortez asked, moving off the sofa and standing behind her.

"Please, you know what they've always thought of me. How low they always treated me."

Cortez pulled her around to face him. "I want you to marry me. *Me,* Julia. Not my family."

"I need time, Cortez. Lots of it."

"Will you change your mind?"

Julia had no answer to that question. "Can we just not talk about this now?" she asked, moving closer to link her arms around his neck. "Can thinking about it be enough?"

Cortez nodded. "For now. For now it can."

* * *

Following the emotional mountain trip, Cortez and Julia immersed themselves in work. For the next two months, Julia was swamped in preliminary tasks in preparation for her show. Cortez was involved with prep for his show as well, but he still had responsibilities to the station in Detroit until the expiration of his contract. Usually it was Cortez who made visits out to California. Julia was quite content with the way things were going. Cortez, on the other hand, was furious.

"What in the world?" Julia whispered when she pulled into her driveway one afternoon to find him there. "You're not due here until next weekend," she said as she stepped out of her Benz.

Cortez lifted himself from the side of his car and walked over to her. "I came for an answer to my question."

Startled, Julia stepped back to assess his seriousness. "I'm not ready to give you one."

"You're not ready to give me one?" he slowly repeated. He crossed his arms over his chest and walked over to her.

"Cortez?" Julia called in a warning tone. She didn't like the determined look on his face one bit.

Grabbing Julia and pulling her close behind him, Cortez led the way to her front door. Choosing not to cause a scene in the driveway, Julia unlocked the door and waited.

"What's the waiting really about, Julia?" he asked when they stepped into the foyer.

Julia blinked at the way Cortez spat the words at her. The cold, deep tone of his voice, however, did not shake her confidence. "So you're tired of waiting, Corky? Well, join the club. I've been waiting for years. It's silly, really, since you were the one who wasn't afraid to take the leap all those years ago. At least you've always had the assurance of knowing that I love you."

"If you love me, then why are you taking so long with this answer of yours?"

Julia rolled her eyes, frustrated by his single train of thought. "I need time to think, damn it!"

"You've had long enough to think!" Cortez said, pointing a finger in her face.

Julia slapped it away. "You jackass! There's no way in hell I'll marry you if I have to be forced into an answer!"

"I'm not forcing you," Cortez argued, his gorgeous eyes narrowing dangerously.

Julia raised her hands in the air. "What the hell do you call it, Cortez? You know, if you want a woman who'll bow and scrape to your every whim or somebody who's socially acceptable and has been raised to your standards, then—"

"Please, Julia! If I wanted that, I'd be with Renee!" Cortez bellowed, wincing as soon as the words left his mouth.

"Go," Julia whispered, turning her back so he couldn't see her tears.

Cortez started to move toward her but stopped himself. "To hell with this," he growled below his breath and stormed out of the house.

Cortez refused to waste any more time in California and returned to Detroit with an invitation in his pocket. The morning after his fight with Julia he found a small, white envelope lying on his office desk. It was an invitation to Darius Kelly's birthday party. Cortez grimaced, rubbing his fingers across the raised print on the card. He knew he'd be there because Julia would be there. Whatever happened between them, he'd never be able to get her out of his mind.

The soft knocking on the door interrupted his thoughts and he turned. When he saw Renee in the doorway he didn't bother to greet her.

Renee took a deep breath and walked inside the room. "I hate this."

Cortez reclined behind his desk and watched her coolly.

"We used to be so close before. Can't we get back to that?"

"We're close enough."

Renee shook her head, searching for a way to break through the wall of ice Cortez had built around himself. "I really think we should try before the audience begins to notice."

Cortez looked up and reared back a bit in his chair. "You know I'm done here once my contract is up."

Renee bristled.

"Good morning, you two," Cora Wallace called in a bright voice as she walked into the office. "I was out and about and thought I'd drop in to check on you," she explained. "I'm happy to see you two together."

Cortez shifted his attention back to his desk. "Don't get too excited, Ma."

Renee couldn't stand it any longer. She ran from the office, before her emotions got the best of her.

Cora leaned against her son's desk. "Baby, how can you—"

"Do you want to be my date for this party?"

Cora frowned. "Party?"

Cortez picked up the invitation and handed it to his mother. "Darius Kelly's birthday party Thursday night."

Cora rolled her eyes. "I don't think so."

"I know Uncle Leon will be there. Ma? Come on now. I need a date to this thing, and it'll really help if she's gorgeous."

Cora smiled and waved her hand at her son. "Stop with the flattery. I'll go. But I do wonder though how you got an invitation to this thing. Or should I even ask?"

Cortez sighed and fiddled with the cuffs of his plum shirt. "Julia didn't invite me. You can bet on it."

"Hmph, right."

Cortez suddenly became too weary to stand or sit behind his desk. He walked across the room and dropped to the suede sofa in the corner.

"Baby?" Cora called, concern for her child etched into her face. "Honey, don't do this to yourself."

"I love her, Ma, very much."

"But look at how hurt you are," Cora whispered.

"If I'm hurt, it's because *I* hurt *her*. So many times. I've finally wised up, and it's too late. She doesn't trust me. She's not playing hard to get, I'd know that. She's genuinely hurt, and I don't blame her. I have to do something to get her to see that I don't look down on her or think she's not good enough. I can't let her get away, but I don't know how to stop it from happening."

Cora listened as Cortez recounted all that had happened between him and Julia. He was so exhausted by the time he was done talking that he drifted off to sleep. For the first time, Cora Wallace had no doubt in her mind that her son truly loved Julia Kelly.

Chapter 21

Julia let herself into her parents' home. They were going to meet her at the airport, but Julia arrived a day earlier than she had planned. She found Tamara and Darius in the dining room. Julia watched them for a long while, enjoying the sight of seeing two people so much in love. The serene look on her face vanished when she realized what they were discussing.

"Daddy! You know?"

Tamara and Darius looked up, screaming when they saw their youngest daughter. Julia was showered with hugs and kisses when they reached her.

"What's going on? I thought Daddy wasn't supposed to know about the party?" Julia asked, frowning at her mother, who looked over at Darius.

"I just decided I wanted to have a hand in it this year."

Tamara rolled her eyes. "Girl, your father's invited everyone he knows, including the Wallaces."

Julia's heart slammed against her chest when she heard the news. "Did I hear that correctly?"

Darius pressed a kiss to Julia's temple. "You know how far me and Cortez's uncle Leon go back. I couldn't invite him and leave out his nephews."

"Why not?" Julia and Tamara asked in unison.

Darius's hearty laugh filled the room and he pulled his wife and daughter close. "It'll be fine, and they probably won't show anyway. Let's stop worrying about this and go out to lunch," he suggested, eyeing the two women hopefully. "I'm paying."

"I still can't believe you're serious," Simon Degerrens said, his freckled face red with worry.

"I am," Cortez assured his station manager, tossing back the rest of his drink.

"You can't do this to me. I'll be ruined if you quit," Simon whined.

"Man, don't overreact." Cortez sighed, shaking his head at Simon, who looked about ready to faint.

"Why would you quit now when you're on top?"

Cortez massaged the bridge of his nose. "I can't think of a better time to go. Plus, with this engagement fiasco, working with Renee is too strange now."

"That's just how it seems," Simon assured him, signaling the waiter for another drink. "You and Renee are professionals. You'll get past it."

"I doubt it. This was in the works long before this whole thing with Renee ever hit the fan," he shared, deciding to be fully honest with the man who'd given him his big shot.

"So that's what all the sudden trips were about?" Simon realized.

Cortez tensed, his brown eyes becoming guarded. "Part of it."

"Cortez, man, listen—"

Smiling, Cortez patted the man's hand. "Thanks, Simon, but the decision has already been made."

On the other side of the same restaurant, Julia and her parents enjoyed mixed drinks.

"Baby girl, are you okay?" Darius asked, noticing the spacey look in Julia's eyes.

Julia smiled and patted her father's hand. "I will be."

"Can we help, honey?" Tamara asked.

"No, it's up to me to get past this."

"Well, what is it?" Darius wanted to know, not liking the defeated sound in his daughter's voice.

Julia groaned and took a sip of her daiquiri. "Cortez asked me to marry him."

"What?" Darius and Tamara sighed.

"What did you tell him?" Tamara asked.

"I told him no, of course. I told him I couldn't put myself through all the ups and downs again with his family—"

"Sweetie, don't let this get you down, you hear?" Tamara said softly, patting her daughter's cheek.

"Oh, I'm not," Julia instantly assured her. "I won't let this beat me. Not again."

Darius leaned back in his chair and regarded his daughter with a thoughtful stare. "You know, baby, if the boy is ready to marry you, maybe you should give him a chance."

"Daddy!"

"Darius!"

Darius shrugged. "I'm just saying that you might want to see where the kid's comin' from."

"Darius, I can't believe you're saying this to her when she's finally got her head on straight."

"What if this were me and you, Tam? Wouldn't you want to give me a chance?"

Tamara threw one arm across her husband's shoulders and gave him a tired look. "Darius, at this moment I don't think you want to hear the answer to that."

Julia's slanting dark eyes darted back and forth between her parents. Suddenly she laughed and her parents followed suit.

"How's everybody doing?"

Julia cut her laughter, thinking she was just hearing things. When she looked up and saw Cortez standing over the table, her heart flew into her throat. Julia knew she missed him, but she had no idea how much until he was right next to her.

"Hello, Cortez," Darius and Tamara spoke, noticing their daughter's silence.

"Why don't you join us, man?" Darius offered, earning a glare from his wife and daughter.

"Thanks, Mr. Kelly," Cortez accepted, unbuttoning the double-breasted sandalwood suit coat he wore.

Julia inched her chair away from Cortez, hoping he couldn't see how affected she was by his presence. Cortez however, was determined to make her aware of how much she wanted him in her life.

"We just ordered some food, Cortez. Have you already eaten?"

Cortez smiled at Darius Kelly. "No, sir, I was having a drink with somebody from work."

Darius was already signaling for the waiter. "We'll get you fixed up, then."

Cortez turned in time to see Julia watching him closely. His wide, sensual lips curved upwards into a knowing smirk. "It was Simon," he informed her, propping the side of his face against his palm.

"Excuse me?" Julia whispered, frowning slightly at his words.

"Who I met here for a drink. It was the station manager for WPDM, Simon Degerrens." He clarified, his warm eyes dropping to her parted lips.

"It's none of my business." Julia looked away from him.

Cortez's knee brushed her thigh in a soft, rhythmic motion. "Yes, it is."

Julia's legs tingled at the erotic twinge that surged through them. She glanced at her parents, but they were in conversation with the waiter. "Why are you doing this?"

"Doing what?" Cortez asked, his expression pure innocence. Replacing his knee with his hand, strong fingers teased the inside of her thigh.

Julia stifled a moan threatening to rise in her throat. Propping her elbow on the table, she massaged the back of her neck.

"Baby? Are you okay?" Tamara asked, noticing the strained look on her daughter's face.

Julia managed a smile for her mother. "Yeah, Ma," she said, covering Cortez's roaming hand with her own. She dug her long nails in, effectively halting his movement. "I'm just fine."

"So, Cortez, are you going to take me up on my invitation?" Darius called across the table.

Cortez nodded and raised his glass to the older man. "Mr. Kelly, I wouldn't miss it for the world."

Chapter 22

Julia unwrapped the silk scarf from her hair and checked for any loose strands. Of course the style was as sleek and shiny as always. It required no further maintenance on her part.

She whispered a curse when the doorbell rang. Slipping into a beige silk robe that rested on the counter, she hurried to the door.

"Oh no, this is not the night for déjà vu," she muttered, once she flung the door open to see Cortez standing on the other side.

Cortez bowed his head as he, too, remembered the night he had come to her hotel room during her last visit. "Can I come in?" he asked.

Julia waved her hand. "What do you want?"

"Don't ask silly questions like that," Cortez advised, walking past her.

Julia slammed her door shut. "Can't you let this go? I

have finally done what you wanted and let go. I can't go back," she sighed, attempting to move past him.

Cortez caught her easily and pulled her around to face him. "Yes, you can."

Julia cleared her throat and stepped away. "You're crazy if you think I want to put myself through that again. Show yourself out, Cork. I have a party to get ready for."

Cortez closed his eyes and asked for the strength to control his temper. Pushing his hands into the deep pockets of his jeans, he followed her into the bedroom.

Julia had already pulled off her robe and was smoothing lotion onto her skin. She saw Cortez behind her in the mirror and whirled around to face him.

"Cut the act, Julia." Cortez moved closer until he was right behind her and pulling her back against him. His caresses were bold as his hands reached around to cup and fondle her breasts. A smile came to his lips when Julia moaned and let her head fall back to his shoulder.

She shivered beneath the tingle of his beard brushing her bare skin. She wanted so much to order him out, but there was no way she could turn away from the pleasure he gave her.

His fingers slid down the smooth, flat plane of her stomach. They played in the mound of black curls shielding her sex. Moving on, he massaged the pad of his finger against the velvety petals of her womanhood.

Julia arched her bare back into the solid wall of Cortez's chest. Her legs shifted farther apart, silently pleading for more of the caress.

Cortez buried his face in her hair and inhaled her scent. He deepened the wicked caress, pressing two fingers into the moist center of her body. Julia moaned, bracing her hands against the edge of the dresser. She squeezed her eyes shut, her hips moving in slow circles.

"Julia…" Cortez groaned, his arousal pressing uncomfortably against the zipper of his jeans. The strokes of his fingers slowed, becoming more sensual. Unable to ignore the demands of his body, he pulled his belt buckle loose and unzipped his jeans.

A gust of air rushed from Julia's throat when she felt the silky, steel length pressed against her back. He cupped her breasts beneath the robe's silky material and buried his face in the side of her neck when she cried out. Tiny curses mingled with those cries as Julia cursed herself for giving in. When she felt him freeing himself, she ground her bottom against his need. Cortez kept one hand cupped around her breast, while the other rooted around in jean pockets for the protection he'd had the forethought to bring along. Once ready, Cortez pulled his fingers away to grasp her thighs and position her to accept him. He groaned as his throbbing length buried deep inside her.

Cortez was hunched over Julia's trembling form. His fists braced on either side of her on the dresser. The force of his thrusts were unyielding, drawing deep moans from them both. Julia raised her arms to encircle Cortez's neck. Her fingers delved into his soft cut hair as she ground her hips against his. They matched each other move for move until their passion was spent. Then they collapsed against the dresser from exhaustion.

A short while later, Cortez and Julia were lying in the huge four-poster oak bed. After another round of lovemaking, they were still intimately connected.

Julia tried to stretch a little beneath the heavy weight of Cortez's body. He felt her move and instantly responded to the unconsciously seductive action. Julia's dark eyes widened when she felt him become hard inside her.

Cortez didn't give her the chance to dwell on it, though. He grasped her hips tightly and made his thrusts slow and deep. It felt as if they loved each other for hours. Afterward, Cortez only gave Julia a moment to recover before he was nibbling her neck and making it clear that he was far from done.

When they finished, Julia closed her eyes and fought the urge to let his touch woo her. Instead, she pulled away from Cortez and left the bed.

"What?" he asked, bracing on his elbow.

"You know, Cortez, if all you want is sex, you can get that from anybody."

Cortez was about to explode when he saw the tears sparkling in Julia's eyes. "Juli, where's all this coming from?" he asked softly, watching her drop to the bed.

"Your family has always been thought of as high society. Someone with a name like that doesn't marry a girl whose father was an underpaid police detective and whose mother worked as a waitress."

"Julia, baby, your mother worked as a waitress to get herself through grad school, and your father now owns a trucking company. He's very well respected now just as he was a long time before that."

Julia turned to face him. "You don't have to tell me that. I love my parents. I'm very proud of them, and I'm proud of myself."

"Then what *is* this?" Cortez asked, desperately trying to remain calm.

"You'll always have doubts about me. You'll always wonder if I'm worth it. You'll wind up hating your family, hating me. You have to know that's why I wouldn't marry you back then...."

Closing his eyes in defeat, Cortez rubbed his fingers through his hair.

"Would you just go? Please?"

As confused as he was agitated, Cortez decided not to push. He left the bed to get dressed. Meanwhile, Julia maintained her seat on the edge of the bed. Cortez watched her as he donned his clothes. Her back was facing him. Still, he could tell that she was crying.

Once dressed, he walked over to the bed and bent down to press a kiss to her shoulder. "I love you," he whispered before leaving.

"Get down, D!" Tamara called, as she watched the scene on the dance floor.

Darius and his lovely daughters were burning up the spot cleared in the spacious living room. The handsome man was a great dancer, he delighted his daughters and guests as he performed the latest dance steps.

Tamara was shaking her head at her family when she heard the front doorbell ring. The graceful, inviting smile on her face vanished when she opened the door.

"Cortez." She greeted him coolly, nodding slightly. She only cast a brief glance at the woman to his left. "Cora," she acknowledged in a flat tone.

Cortez bowed his head, a smirk tugging at his mouth. "Can you two try getting along for a change?"

"Why?" both women questioned at once.

"Because you need to," Cortez told them, walking on into the house. He was drawn to the crowd in the center of the living room. Seeing Julia there with her father and sister, he couldn't look away.

"Well, Cora, are you coming in or staying out here on the porch?" Tamara asked, none too gently.

Cora sighed and stepped inside. Her eyes roamed the lovely, comfortable interior of the home. Of course, she would never compliment it. "I tell you, Tam, your parties haven't changed a bit. They're always so…laid-back."

Tamara propped her hands on her hips. She knew the comment wasn't mean to be flattering. Sighing, she looked out into the party.

"You know, Cora, I haven't liked you since high school," she said, hearing the woman's sharp gasp at her words. "I know the feeling's mutual, so there's no need to pretend."

Cora shrugged, acknowledging the statement. "I still wonder why it's so important to my son, though?"

Tamara took a deep breath and watched Cortez staring at Julia. "I've got an idea," she said.

The trio of Kellys finally gave the other guests a chance to flex their dancing legs. Julia headed to the buffet table for a glass of champagne.

"Y'all looked good out there."

Julia's fingers tightened around the stem of her glass when she heard Correll Wallace's voice behind her. She turned around slowly. "What the hell are you doing here?"

Correll turned toward Darius, who was talking with his uncle Leon and Cora. "Your pop invited me."

"Hmph. Something I'll never understand."

"Look, Julia, I really wanted to come here and apologize."

"Save it."

"I can't. This crap has been eating away at me since it happened. I should've never gone along with it."

"It didn't take much to convince you, though, did it?"

"I hate like hell that it happened."

Julia rolled her eyes. "Just get away from me, all right?"

Correll started to walk off but hesitated. "Julia, I hope you can forgive me."

Losing what little control she had over her temper, Julia splashed the rest of her champagne in Correll's face. "You have no idea what I went through because of you! If you did, there is no way in hell you'd ask me to forgive you."

Cortez witnessed the scene between his brother and Julia. When he saw her throw the champagne in Correll's face and turn away he knew he had to act immediately. Scanning the room, he located the DJ booth and headed over.

Julia's heels clicked on the hardwood floors as she headed out of the room. *I have to get out of here before these people drive me crazy!* she almost screamed.

"Can I have everyone's attention for a moment, please?" Cortez called into the mic. He waited for Julia to walk back into the room before he continued.

In a daze, Julia returned. She watched him with great interest, as did everyone else in the room.

A satisfied smile came to Cortez's face when he saw Julia. "Thanks, I'll make this brief. I need to tell you all what's happened to me. It involves a lady all of you know. She's beautiful, smart and I love her. Took me a long time to admit that. I love her more than my life. I trust her with my life and my heart. There's nothing anyone could ever say or do to change that. I was stupid. I know that. I told her time and time again how I felt, but she doesn't believe me, though I can't say I blame her. And on top of that, she thinks she doesn't fit into my world. She thinks she's not good enough. I don't know how that can be since she's the best thing I know. I love you, Julia, and I want to spend the rest of my life showing you how much. If you'll let me." Clearing his throat, Cortez set the mic down and made his way through the silent crowd.

Julia stood rooted to her spot, waiting for him to close the distance. When he stood before her, she took a moment to raise her eyes to his. Cortez cupped her face in his large hands and brushed his lips across hers.

"We need to talk," Cortez told her, sighing with relief when she nodded.

As the couple headed upstairs, the silence downstairs turned alive with excited conversation.

"Have you lost your mind?" Julia asked in a hushed voice when they reached her old bedroom.

"I promise I haven't."

Julia propped the side of her face against her palm. "You wanna tell me what just happened down there?"

Cortez stroked the light shadow darkening his face and took a seat on the bed. "What happened down there had a lot to do with me trying to prove how much I love you and want you to be with me."

"I believe that," Julia told him, sitting on the bed, as well. "I believed that before you did...all this. I can't forget what was said in California, though, or what's happened since I've come back to Detroit. I can't go through life wondering if you trust me to say the appropriate thing or whether I'm coming across too strong or if aspects of my personality will dictate your level of trust."

Now Cortez closed his eyes as realization hit him. "Is this why you couldn't give me an answer, Juli? Is it what really fueled your decision not to work on the show together?"

Julia was already shaking her head. "I would've taken issue with that regardless." She leaned over, bracing her elbows to her knees. "L.A. lives on gossip, and while we've got a lot of competition, you can best believe the two of us would've made for some juicy stories."

"Damn right," Cortez muttered almost proudly, clearing his throat when she looked his way.

"As for your proposal," she kept her eyes on his, "yes, that had everything to do with why I stalled on answering." She exhaled as if a weight were lifted with the confession. "I love you," she said, brushing the back of her hand across his. "I know you love me, but unlike *my* love, yours is set on a foundation of requirements."

"Juli—"

"Be honest with me now and admit it." Her eyes were suddenly ablaze with emotion. "The only reason you came back to L.A. was because you discovered Correll had lied about what happened."

Cortez ground on his jaw until it ached. "Am I glad you didn't have sex with my brother? God yes." He stood. "And was what he did wrong? Absolutely. None of it was your fault and I realized that as long as I had you back that was *all* that mattered."

Julia's eyes wavered in disbelief and she bowed her head.

"Now who's having a problem with trust?" Cortez challenged as he watched her.

Julia opened her mouth to explain and closed it when she couldn't. Frustrated then, she stood and smoothed her hands over the tight sleeves of her black jumpsuit while she paced.

Cortez crossed the room, taking her by the hand and pressing her back to the nearest wall. "It didn't matter, Julia. That's the truth, I swear it. I tried to tell you that, but you wouldn't take my call."

Julia blinked then as memory of the call to her office hit her like a rush of cold wind.

Cortez graced her with a knowing smile. "I guess I should have told Lexi more about why I called, but I didn't think you wanted her knowing quite that much."

Her fingers curved into the front of his shirt. "So you were calling to—"

"I was calling to ask you to forgive me for being the biggest idiot in the world and for hurting you so many times." He cupped his hands around her neck. "I called to tell you that you've got my heart, mind and body. I called to tell you I love you, Julia Kelly."

Determined not to let the words turn her into a blubbering mess, she pressed her lips together and took a shuddery breath. "When did you talk to Correll?"

"I went to his office right after the call. I was pissed off as hell and went in there intending to rough him up," he managed to say without getting upset at the memory. "I decided instead to ask him for the truth, and he gave it to me. If you must know, hearing the truth made me feel like an even bigger idiot. Listen, Julia, I'll do whatever you say to prove how serious I am." His lips met hers and he pressed ever so gently. "Only please don't say go."

Julia's attempt at suppressing her emotions was hopeless when he kissed both corners of her mouth.

"I love you," he whispered. "I love you." A low growl sounded in his throat when he felt Julia soften in his arms. "Will you marry me now?"

The words caused Julia's body to stiffen and she shivered slightly. Cortez pulled away and cupped her chin in his hand.

"Do you love me?"

"You know I do. I love you more than anything. I just don't want to get hurt again," she admitted softly.

Cortez nodded, the look in his brown eyes soft and warm. "Honey, I can't promise that won't happen."

"I know—"

"But I did just declare my love in front of a lot of people I know. I assure you I'm not looking to get hurt, either. I'll chance it for you, Julia. I'll chance anything for you."

Julia's heart skipped at the words. "You want to marry me after all this time," she whispered, feeling lightheaded.

Cortez chuckled. "And I was crazy enough to almost let you get away from me twice."

They were silent for a while, each taking in all that had occurred that evening. After a moment, Julia smiled and allowed herself to melt into another of Cortez's mind-numbing kisses. "Now what?" she asked, once he'd released her lips.

Cortez leaned close again. "Now we get married."

Julia tilted her head and watched him curiously. "You already have a date in mind, don't you?"

"Tomorrow."

Tears filled her eyes as she laughed. "Tomorrow? Don't you at least want to take time to—"

"Uh-uh," he refused, walking his fingers across the fabric of her outfit. "I've taken enough time. All I want to do now is take my wife. Besides, it's already been planned."

Julia's tears of laughter mingled with tears of elation. "Cortez! I can't believe you already... When did you... How did you know I would finally say yes?"

"Let's just say I had a good feeling about it," Cortez said, smiling.

Julia smiled back, wiping a tear from her eye before kissing the man she loved. She looked into his eyes as she thought that this wasn't as good as the first time. It was even better.

* * * * *

REQUEST YOUR FREE BOOKS!

2 FREE NOVELS
PLUS 2 *FREE GIFTS!*

KIMANI™ ROMANCE

Love's ultimate destination!

KROM10R

THE *MATCH MADE* SERIES

**Melanie Harte's exclusive matchmaking service—
The Platinum Society—can help any soul find their
ideal mate. Because when love is perfect,
it is a match made in heaven...**

Book #1
by *Essence* Bestselling Author
ADRIANNE BYRD
Heart's ♡ *Secret*
June 2010

Book #2
by National Bestselling Author
CELESTE O. NORFLEET
Heart's ♡ *Choice*
July 2010

Book #3
by *Essence* Bestselling Author
DONNA HILL
Heart's ♡ *Reward*
August 2010

www.kimanipress.com
www.myspace.com/kimanipress

KPMMSP

L❤VE IN THE LIMELIGHT

Fantasy, Fame and Fortune...Hollywood-Style!

Book #1
By *New York Times* and *USA TODAY*
Bestselling Author Brenda Jackson
STAR OF HIS HEART
August 2010

Book #2
By A.C. Arthur
SING YOUR PLEASURE
September 2010

Book #3
By Ann Christopher
SEDUCED ON THE RED CARPET
October 2010

Book #4
By *Essence* Bestselling Author Adrianne Byrd
LOVERS PREMIERE
November 2010

Set in Hollywood's entertainment industry,
two unstoppable sisters and their two friends
find romance, glamour and dreams-come-true.